THE WOMAN
AT THE WINDOW

MARGO MYSTERIES

THE WOMAN
AT THE WINDOW

J. B. JENKINS

Thomas Nelson Publishers
Nashville

Published in Nashville, Tennessee, by Thomas
Nelson, Inc., and distributed in Canada by
Lawson Falle, Ltd., Cambridge, Ontario.

**Library of Congress
Cataloging-in-Publication Data**

Jenkins, Jerry B.
   [Margo]
   The woman at the window / J. B. Jenkins.
     p.   cm. — (Margo mysteries : vol. 1)
   Previously published as: Margo, c1980.
   ISBN 0-8407-3209-0
   I. Title. II. Series: Jenkins, Jerry B.
  Margo mysteries : vol. 1.
  PS3560.E485W66 1991
  813'.54—dc20   90–45015
                        CIP

Printed in the United States of America
1 2 3 4 5 6 7 — 96 95 94 93 92 91

THE WOMAN
AT THE WINDOW

ONE

They say more women than men attempt suicide, but that more men are successful. I guess women are just attention-seekers. That's why I couldn't figure out this girl. Hers was an attempt without observers.

I had just finished a fairly successful job interview and had reason to believe I might be working in the Atlanta Tower as a commercial artist within a couple of weeks. Maybe not, though. Someone would be bound to recognize me as the jerk who couldn't even find his way back to the elevator.

For sure no one would recognize me as Philip Spence, the hero who kept a girl from committing suicide. No one knew. It was one weird suicide attempt.

In looking for the elevator I found myself in a little hallway, one of those meaningless crannies you find when you're lost in a skyscraper. It leads to a window—that's all. Maybe it was the architect's joke.

I spun around to head back to the main corridor, and there she was. I almost ran into her. "This is a great place for meditating," I joked.

She said nothing, but she looked as if I had offended her. That irritated me. I mean, the place wasn't private or anything. I let the million-dollar question spew forth: "What are you doing here?"

She ignored the question. "Do you have to be here now?" she asked. I was surprised at how feminine she sounded, despite her disposition.

"I guess not, if you're busy," I said. I wanted to see her smile, or at least loosen up. "Is there much to do here?"

She just sighed. No smile. Trembling, she drew her clenched fists slowly to her face. Suddenly I didn't feel so funny.

"Hey, listen, what's wrong?" I asked. "Are you hiding from someone?"

"No," she said, annoyed. "I'm trying to get up enough courage to jump out that window." I knew the window was there, but for some reason I turned to look.

No crowd, no public drama. *She's serious,* I thought.

"If there was one place I didn't expect to see anyone, it was here," she said, crying.

I decided to challenge her, to make her see that she didn't really want to go through with it. "The window isn't even open," I taunted. "What are you gonna do, run through the glass?" I let that image dance on my brain for a few seconds. She'd have made a real mess in the alley thirty floors below.

My strategy didn't work. She was becoming even more determined, staring at the window. "Do you want me to open it?" I asked.

"Would you?" she said softly, as if it would be the kindest thing I could do and she'd be ever so grateful.

"Hey, come on now," I said. "What's the problem?"

She grew cold again. "If I'd wanted to tell my story, I'd have left a note," she snapped. "Open the window."

Well, she had no idea how to open the huge thing, and there was no way she was going to go through safety glass. She pushed at the window angrily.

So I opened it. Not because I wanted her to jump, of course, but because something told me that this girl was going to have to choose to live by turning down a bona fide opportunity to die.

The dirty Atlanta air blew in. I turned to her and motioned like an usher toward the window. She didn't move except to shiver. When she took a half step toward the window, I decided not to block her path. She stopped.

"Leave," she said.

I couldn't. I could do all the rest. I could tell her to go ahead, and I could challenge her, and I could try my amateur psychology on her, but I would never have been able to live with myself if I had left her to jump.

"You know I could keep you from jumping," I lied. "All I would have to do is grab you and take you away from the window." I'm not a big guy, but I think I convinced her.

"But you won't stop me, will you?" she pleaded.

"What will I tell the reporters? That I didn't even try to talk you out of it?"

"I have no reason to live!" She was shouting now.

"Do you have a reason to die?"

"Having no reason to live is reason enough to die," she said. It was ominous. A truism. I had no answer.

There was silence for more than a minute. Then I started talking, saying things I hadn't thought about saying.

"What if you knew somebody loved you?" I began.

"No one does," she said.

I could hardly hear her.

"Not my family. No one here at work. No one anywhere."

"Someone cares," I said. "God cares." I hadn't said anything like that since high school when I had come back from a youth retreat all fired up.

But now it wasn't an obligation. I wanted more than anything to convince this girl that God loved her.

I hadn't cried in front of anyone since I was twelve years old, but I didn't care. She was looking at me now, straight into my eyes. "Listen," I pleaded.

She walked past me toward the window and stood staring at the floor, chin tucked tightly to her chest. Putting both hands on the edge of the window, she tried to slide it shut. No way. She looked at me with a helpless smile. I helped her close it.

"I'd have never guessed you for a *Margo*," I said. We were in the second-floor coffee shop where she worked. "Ready to talk yet?" She shook her head. "At least tell me this," I said.

"Why did you wait until you were off work to head for the window?"

She shrugged. She wouldn't even look at me.

"You're not going to tell me about it, are you?" I said, resigning myself to it. I felt a little guilty about being so curious, but it's not every day I encounter a suicidal waitress.

"I don't know yet," she said.

Two of her waitress friends stopped by to ask if she was all right. She nodded to each. They looked at me warily.

"See?" I said. "People care. Your friends care."

She looked as if she wished I hadn't talked her out of jumping. "They don't care at all," she said quickly in a whisper. "What else could they say to someone who's sitting here crying in her coffee? Anyway, they'd just love to have something to talk about."

"You're really a case, you know that?" I said, shaking my head the way a mother might over a kid who has sloshed home through every puddle. Margo didn't take it that way.

"Thanks a lot," she said. "You know, for a while I thought you really cared."

Now I was offended. I wanted to blast her for messing up my day. I had been elated to find that God could use me to share His love with someone, and I had been glad to help. I hadn't even minded that this girl thought of no one but herself, never asking whether I really had the time to baby her.

"What do you want?" I asked. "Really, what do you want?" I tried to sound as sincere as possible. I figured I was at least entitled to hear her tale of woe, and I for sure wouldn't get to if she thought I resented her taking my time. I really wanted to explain to her what God could mean to her, but she was hardly in the mood for that yet.

"Do you really want to help?" she asked. "Right now, I mean."

I nodded tentatively. I'd have bet my life she was going to ask me to leave her alone. Wrong.

"I would like to talk about anything but today," she said

deliberately, as if she had thought it out for a long time. She even stopped crying and became surprisingly articulate. "I'm not ready for your sermon," she said, raising her eyebrows as if to assure me that she hadn't intended that to be a low blow, "but I would like you to just tell me about yourself. If you don't want to talk to me, I'll understand."

More self-pity, I thought.

She read my mind. "No," she said. "Really. It's not fair of me to be so mysterious, and I appreciate what you did for me up there. I'm not ready to talk about it. Can you just talk to me and not be offended if I happen to look bored or don't seem to listen?"

"I could," I said, "but I might not enjoy it." Her jewelry, simple and expensive, told me she wasn't just another coffee shop waitress looking for some bucks before moving on.

"You're not really a waitress at heart, are you?" I asked.

She was staring out the window. "I said I wanted *you* to talk," she said. "Could we please just save my story?"

"I will get to hear about you then?"

"Yes. I don't know . . ."

"Margo, listen. I've known you for what, a half hour? I don't know anything about you except that you really wanted to kill yourself a little while ago. Needless to say, I'm not experienced in this, but I have to believe you want to be alone right now."

"No. You're right that I really don't feel like talking *or* listening, but I don't want to be alone."

Obviously, I couldn't stay with her indefinitely. "Why don't you go home and try to relax?" I said. "Here's the phone number at my apartment. My name's Philip Spence, and if you need something, you can call me any time of the day or night."

She didn't like it, but I think she realized there were no other options. "Are you going to be all right?" I asked as I slid out of the booth. She pressed her lips tight and nodded. She was crying by the time I left the coffee shop.

All the way to my apartment I pondered why I had made myself available to her. Was it because I cared? Or because God was caring through me? Or because there was simply no other choice? Who would leave someone helpless? Maybe I had just been courteous. I had done the only right thing, hadn't I?

My apartment, which doubled for an office from which I worked on and sold my free-lance illustrations, was as homey as it could be without a family. I had been getting by free-lancing, but that was because the apartment was my only major expense. With the economy as it was, I had been scouting for a full-time commercial art job, one that would leave me time to free-lance in the evenings if I wished, yet pay enough so I wouldn't have to if I didn't want to.

I had gone the sensible route for my interview that day, guessing at the conservatism of my potential employer in this Southern city. I wound up looking more conservative than Mr. Willoughby did. Owners of art studios and advertising agencies can afford to wear casual jackets and no ties, I guess.

He seemed impressed with my work, even if my suit had thrown him a bit. He would be calling me within a few days about a staff job as an illustrator. My parents would love it. They had always been suspicious of my free-lancing, though I had made a lot of money in each of the last two years. "Why don't you get a job?" my mother often asked. "And why don't you find one here closer to Dayton?"

There were good people. I had written to Mom about looking for a full-time job. My free-lance accounts, good as they were, could end in a week if budgets needed tightening. The loss of one good account could mean a third of my income. I needed money now and for the future. Somehow I knew in the back of my mind that "just the right girl would come along," the way Mom always said. I didn't enjoy living alone, and while my only serious romance had ended in disappointment in college, I looked forward to what I hoped was inevitable.

The phone took me from my half-eaten steak. *It might be Margo.* I let it ring again to collect my thoughts. *What if she's just slashed her wrists? I'll wish I'd stayed with her.*

It was long distance from Dayton. "How'd it go?" Mom asked. "Did you get a job?"

"Not yet," I said. "But maybe."

"Oh, I hope not," she said. "Try here in Dayton. You've made a name for yourself. People here know you're good. You know Carl Ferguson could use a good artist." We'd been through it before.

"I know, Mom. I appreciate it. Maybe if nothing turns up here."

"Have you been going to church?" she asked suddenly, characteristically changing the subject.

"Oh, not as much as I should," I admitted. Not for months, was the truth. I had no excuse. I just slept in on Sundays.

"No better place to meet a girl than in church," Mom said.

"That's a fact," I agreed. "You wouldn't believe where I met a girl today."

Mom didn't know whether to be excited or skeptical. She wanted me to meet girls, but until she knew where I'd met one, she wasn't about to sound enthusiastic.

I told her all about Margo. She was thrilled that I had told Margo about Christ. She even had Dad listen in on the extension phone. I must say I was glad to be able to tell them about it, as a sort of absolution for having been so lax in my church and general spiritual life, and for insinuating to Mom that I had been to church even off and on lately.

When I finally hung up, my steak was cold and my Coke was warm. I threw the steak back on the broiler as the phone rang again.

"I've been trying to reach you for an hour," Margo said.

I suppose I should have felt guilty for not having kept my

phone open for Margo's call. I didn't. What did she expect—
an apology? How was I supposed to know she'd call right
away?

"I had a long distance call from home," I explained.

"I need to see you," she said.

"From my parents," I said.

"Can you get away soon?" she asked.

"In Dayton, Ohio," I said.

"You're not listening," she whined.

"Oh, really? OK, where do you want to meet? At the coffee
shop?"

"That's all I need," she said. "To be seen with you there
again. The rumors would never quit."

We settled on an all-night restaurant about halfway between our apartments. It was a twenty-minute drive, giving
me time to guess whether Margo would be in the mood for
talking or for listening.

She could have listened by phone, I decided. Maybe she
was ready to tell me, in person, what had caused her to consider suicide.

TWO

"You'll never understand, Philip," Margo said at the restaurant, "but as soon as I quit crying and went home, I stuffed myself."

"You're right, I don't understand. I would've been too upset to eat."

"That's what I mean about not understanding. I eat when I'm upset."

"And now you want to eat again?"

"Yes."

"I'm not your father. Go ahead and order."

"Eat something with me?"

"No, I had a steak—at—oh, no. I've got half a steak burning in the oven! I've got to go."

"No, you don't. How high is your oven turned?"

"About three hundred," I said.

"It won't be any more burned by the time you get home than it is already. And it won't start a fire."

She ordered, and the waitress pretended not to mind that I wasn't having anything. She even said it was OK if we sat and talked awhile. She didn't know how long "awhile" was going to be. Neither did I.

It didn't do much for Margo's ego, but I yawned through much of her story. Not that the story was boring, but it was late, and I'd had a full day.

"You don't want to hear this," she'd say every few sentences.

"No, really, I do," I'd say through a yawn.

I'd been right about her not being just another waitress looking for quick cash. She was from a well-to-do Chicago family, and she was the daughter of a judge. I really wasn't ready for the next bit of news; her *mother* was the judge.

The way she ate made me hungry. Margo went on trying to tell me her life story while I looked around for the waitress.

Her story was depressing and totally humorless. She'd been popular through grade school and the first couple of months of high school. Then she suspected her mother was seeing another man. Her parents' marriage had been only cordial for about three years, and Margo had sensed something was wrong, though she didn't understand what it was.

"The change was so gradual it sneaked up on me," she said. "I'm not sure just when I realized that they didn't seem to love each other anymore. They were compassionate to me all right, but they showed more affection to me than to each other. They couldn't have known how it hurt me.

"I found myself dreaming of the good old days. I'd see Mr. and Mrs. Virginia Franklin, sleeping in separate rooms and treating each other more like neighbors than spouses, and I'd cry myself to sleep. All I could think of was my childhood. Trips to the zoo with Mommy and Daddy. Being carried when I was too tired to walk. Seeing them look into each other's eyes and smile."

Margo talked of the autumn of 1963 with particular pain, and I felt as if I were intruding on her history.

"I remember the coming-out party my parents threw for me," she said. "It was everything my suburban Winnetka friends expected, according to the *Chicago Tribune* social page. I was a freshman in high school then, but the football games, homecoming, and being a debutante left me cold. I wanted our family happy again."

She had been a reader of novels and classic romances and began to dream of a guy who would sweep her off her feet and somehow replace the security she was losing as her family fell apart.

"By November I was no longer smiling, and everyone noticed, especially the guys. Mike Grantham broke the news to me about President Kennedy's assassination. He was so sensitive, so caring. I hoped he would invite me to the Christmas

Ball, but by then I had become depressed and irritable. My status as the daughter of a hundred-thousand-dollar-a-year garment executive and a judge suddenly meant little to the 'in' crowd."

I looked around again for the waitress and finally caught her eye. "We can save the rest," Margo said.

"No way," I said. "I've invested this much time, I want it all." While I ate, Margo kept talking.

"At first, I had little to go on in suspecting my mother had a lover, but it was enough. I basically knew when she had trials scheduled, and everyone knew when the big social events would demand her appearance. But Mom was gone too much at other times—like during the early evening—and she was always coming home late. I asked Dad about it and told him it could only mean she was seeing another man. That hurt him and I was almost sorry I had mentioned it. He confronted her, and she denied it. He believed her. I didn't.

"Still, the marriage was over. Mom and Dad were seldom seen together socially, and by the end of my sophomore year, Dad had moved out. I was crushed."

"Whatever happened with Mike what's-his-name?"

"Nothing. We chatted between classes now and then, but a mealy-mouthed, shy math major took me to the prom, and I had the feeling we were doing each other a favor—his asking and my accepting, I mean. When I closed my eyes, I was dancing with Mike."

"Who was Mike dancing with?"

"Whoever he wanted. Bouncy, skinny cheerleaders."

"Did your parents ever get divorced?"

"Yes, and I was more disgraced than my mother. She talked to me only to hassle me about my appearance, and I talked to her only to accuse her of cheating on Dad. It was a cold war."

"Did you know for sure she was seeing someone else?"

"Oh, sure. She argued on the phone often with a man she called Richard."

"Did she know you knew?"

"No, I really don't think she did, and I've always thought she was incredibly naive about that, especially for a judge."

"Did you ever find out who this Richard was?"

"You're getting ahead of me."

"Sorry." I was just trying to hurry the thing along. It was interesting, like I say, but I couldn't really see the link between a divorce ten years ago and a suicide attempt today.

"My dad visited me now and then, and he chose to respect, admire, and believe Mom. He decided the love was simply gone and was quite content to believe there was no other man. I resented that I got only a half-hour chat with him every few weeks, so when I was a senior I staged a suicide attempt."

It was Margo's first and last attention-getting effort. To me it was one of the most transparent cries for help I had ever heard of. Even Margo had to fight a smile as she told it. "Daddy had called and asked if he could visit me while Mother was working one day. I said yes, hung up, and downed thirty aspirins. Then I sprawled on the living room floor with the empty bottle in my hand and was conveniently (and violently) ill when he arrived forty-five minutes later."

"He obviously saw it for what it was," I commented.

"Not at first. He couldn't put it together, and I still regret that. All he could do was assume that his visit had somehow pushed me to attempt suicide."

"But you got his attention?"

"Oh, yes. And I've fantasized a thousand times since, remembering Daddy carrying me to his car and racing me to the hospital. Even as sick as I was, I wouldn't have traded the experience for anything. I was Daddy's for several hours."

"Did you talk?"

"Yes, but I couldn't bring myself to talk about Richard. Mother had been arguing with him on the phone nearly every day. I was sure they were fighting and that they might break up. That gave me hope Mother and Daddy would get back together. From what Daddy said, though, I knew he still chose to believe there was no other man."

"How did your mother react to the aspirin bit?"

"Oh, that really did it between us. She became openly hostile. Once she told me she wished she had a daughter to show off at social events. That really hurt, as you can imagine.

"She begged me not to tell anyone about the aspirins. I would have loved to have told everyone, just to disgrace her, but I was embarrassed about it too. I finished high school with no more dates—not even with the math major—and grades that qualified me only for a local junior college."

"Did you go?"

"No. No one from Winnetka, and certainly not the daughter of Virginia Franklin, went anywhere less prestigious than Northwestern University, so I went nowhere. I worked at the public library, read, slept, ate, fought with Mother, and prayed that Mike Grantham was still single."

"Did you really think you had a chance with him?"

"Don't forget my reading, Philip. I read stories where the girl always got her man. I was enchanted with the South, and I planned to run off one day to Atlanta, develop some charm, and return to look up Mike. Somehow, in my daydream, I always thought of him as Michael. My biggest dread was that I would run into him before I got my head straight."

"Did that ever happen?"

"I'm getting to that."

"Sorry," I yawned.

"One day late in 1970 I answered the phone while Mother was outside for a few minutes. It was Richard, only he thought he was talking to Mother. 'Virginia,' he said, 'this is Richard. Can you come to Inverness right away?'"

"Did he ever realize he was talking to you and not your mother?"

"No. I just said, 'Sure,' and he hung up. Then mother came in."

"Wait. Now, did his talking about Inverness give you any clue to who he was?"

"Yes, I guessed almost immediately from reading the papers every day. It was only a hunch, but the assistant state's attorney, Richard Wanmacher, was from Inverness, a smaller town but every bit as exclusive as Winnetka. I had never put it together with Mother's Richard."

"Were you sure now?"

"Not until Mother came in. As matter-of-factly as possible, I told her that a Richard from Inverness had called and wanted her to come there right away. I don't know how long it had been since I had seen her blow her cool. She flushed and bristled and said, 'Nonsense, I don't know anyone from Inverness.' I said, 'Maybe it was that guy from the state's attorney's office who lives out there.' And she said, 'Oh, well, yes, perhaps.'"

"Wow."

"You haven't heard anything yet, Philip." Margo said. "Mom made a quick call from the kitchen phone when she thought I was in my room. I wasn't. I was on the stairs listening. Mother was hissing into the phone like a snake. 'I'll kill you, Richard. Don't think I won't,' she was saying. It was something about his even thinking of staying with his wife after all of his promises to Mother.

"That night I knew I hated her. From then on it was hard to think of her in a good light, even in childhood memories. I began to dream exclusively of Michael and me and our future . . . ."

"Well?" I said after a minute of silence.

"I'm tired," Margo said.

"You ought to be. It's one A.M. But I want to hear what happened."

She looked at me coldly. I knew her well by now, what she dreamed about, what hurt her, what she wanted in life. At least, I thought I knew.

"I'm talked out," she said flatly, staring past me.

"Are you sure?" I said, "Or have you just come to the part that's hardest to talk about?"

"You guessed it," she said, making a stab at sounding light.

"Do you want me to talk you into it?"

She laughed a pitiful laugh. "That was a good question. You're as sensitive as I always dreamed Michael would be."

I shot her a double take.

"Oh, don't read anything into that," she said. "Really, as much as I admire you for listening to me and for caring, I'm smart enough not to go falling for you."

I feigned offense. "And what is *that* supposed to mean?"

"You know," she said, smiling. Then she was serious. "For one thing, I know how to protect myself from pain, in spite of my somewhat fanciful dreams."

I debated badgering her to tell me the painful part of the story, but I somehow sensed there were two parts to it. First there was whatever was so painful at home nine years ago. Then there was whatever had pushed her past the brink and forced her to that window on the thirtieth floor today—well, yesterday now.

Margo saved me the begging. "I want to finish this tonight," she said.

"This morning," I corrected. "And don't forget the former steak in my oven." She didn't smile.

"Mother killed Richard Wanmacher," she said.

I was speechless. "How in the world do you know that?" I finally managed.

"Mother slammed the phone down after talking with him that night, ran upstairs, rustled through some drawers, ran back down, and sped off."

"To Inverness?"

"Where else? When I woke up the next morning, she was on her way out the door to head for court in Chicago. I'll never forget the headline in the paper . . . ."

Margo's voice trailed off. She paled. I waited, but I didn't ask.

" 'Assistant State's Attorney Slain; Wife Charged,' " she said slowly.

"Wanmacher's wife was charged?"

"Isn't that ironic? The only motive ever suggested was that she suspected he was seeing another woman. Mrs. Wanmacher admitted that was true, but she never said who the woman might be, and the press had no idea either."

"Your mother's name never got into it?"

"Never. Mrs. Wanmacher maintained her innocence and fought the charge for three years."

"Was she innocent?"

"Of course! I told you, Mother did it."

"How can you be so sure?" I asked.

"For one thing, the gun. Richard was shot through the eye from a foot away with a twenty-two caliber pistol. It was the pistol in Daddy's dresser that I was never supposed to touch as a child."

"How do you know it was that gun?"

"Because as soon as I read the story in the paper, I looked for the gun. It was gone."

"You know that doesn't prove a thing."

"Maybe it doesn't prove anything legally, but I'll bet if that gun were found, it could be proved."

"You don't know your mother went to see Wanmacher. You can't even be sure you talked to Wanmacher. It could have been coincidental that a Richard from Inverness called your mother."

"But you agree the odds are that it was the same Richard she had been arguing with by phone for weeks?"

"OK, I'll buy that."

"Then it was probably her lover," Margo said.

"Probably."

"I'm saying her lover was Wanmacher."

"Why?"

"Because after his death, the phone calls stopped. She was

left with no one. Not Daddy. Not me. Not Richard. She even tried to get close to me. That proves she was desperate."

I sat staring.

She continued, "When Mother reached out to me, I found myself hating her more. I told her once that I knew about Richard. She covered well. Then I asked her where Daddy's gun was. She said she thought he had taken it with him and that she hadn't seen it for ages."

"Is that possible?"

"I asked Daddy, without telling him why I was asking, 'Whatever happened to that gun you used to keep in the bedroom?' 'It's probably still there,' he said."

"You didn't tell your father?" I said.

"Are you kidding? He chose to believe there was no other man, and I'm supposed to tell him that there not only was, but that Mother murdered him?"

"Who did you tell?"

Margo said nothing. She shoved her plates aside and went to the washroom. When she returned I asked her again.

"Who did you tell?"

"Only you, Philip," she said.

I shook my head violently. "You're putting me on," I said. "You hate your mother, and you have reason to believe she killed a man, and yet you tell no one?"

"You forget that I love Daddy. This would destroy him."

"And it would eliminate the possibilities of your dream-world Michael too, wouldn't it? Who would want the daughter of a murderer?"

"I thought of that too."

"Incredible."

The waitress came to clear the table. "My shift is over," she said. "You can stay, but can I give you your check now?"

"Sure," I said. Margo took it as her cue to head for her car. I paid the check and caught up.

"I still don't know how you got to Atlanta, or what happened today—nine years after the murder—to make you flip out."

"Flip out?" she said, walking quickly.

"Wrong term," I admitted, "but remember where we met."

Margo stopped and thrust her hands deep into her coat pockets. Rain began to fall gently, and right there on Peachtree Drive in Atlanta, more of the story spilled out.

"I kept badgering Mother about Richard and the gun, never actually using the name Wanmacher and never actually accusing. She knew I had no evidence, so she continued to brush it off. But she did begin encouraging me to get out on my own. She even decided to finance my venture to Atlanta. She paid for my flight here and sent me the money to buy a car and get set in an apartment.

"I took the money that time, but I told her that I couldn't take any more. I started sending her checks back, but she wrote and told me she was putting them in my account for whenever I needed the money. When I got my job, I started paying her back for the trip and car, but she's never cashed the checks."

I shivered. We leaned against a building. "Go on," I said.

"You're tired," she said. "And so am I. Should we pick this up somewhere tomorrow?"

"No. If you don't want to talk about it, I understand. But if you're only thinking of my fatigue, forget it. I'm already functioning on automatic, and my apartment must smell like a charcoal grill. Why don't you ride with me there so I can turn the oven off? We can talk on the way, and then I'll bring you back here to your car."

"You aren't going to try to take liberties, are you?" she said as we walked to the car. We both laughed for the first time since we'd met.

In the car her sense of humor vanished. "I haven't talked to Mother for over a year, and except to send me bank deposit receipts, she hasn't written to me either. I have corresponded with Daddy every few months, but it's been on the surface. I figured if Mother could stay on the bench with murder on her conscience, I could pretend I never knew her."

"How about your dreams of Michael?"

With that she broke down and sobbed. I drove to my apartment and ran up to turn off the oven. The place was pretty smoky. I opened the windows and went back to the car. It was raining hard now.

The car windows fogged us into our own world. Margo cried as she talked, and I worried that all this honesty had backfired. Instead of releasing her from the haunting thoughts that led to our first encounter, my compassionate listening had brought her right back to where she'd been. "You don't have to tell me tonight," I said.

"I want to now."

"OK."

She spoke slowly and deliberately. "Since I left home I've dreamed about Michael during the day and the murder at night. I can see Mother pulling into Richard Wanmacher's driveway, and him coming to meet her as she gets out of her car. He gets right up to her when she shoves the twenty-two in his face and fires—"

"You sound as if you were there."

"After hearing Mrs. Wanmacher tell of her husband walking out of the house to his death, I can picture it perfectly."

"She saw the murder?"

"Yes, but not the murderer. Mother met him between her car door and the headlights, and the lights blocked Mrs. Wanmacher's view of her."

"You're still talking about nine years ago, Margo. What happened today?"

"This happens to me every day! Don't you understand?"

I nodded. "Whatever happened in the case?"

"After several years of continuances, mistrials, and changes of venue, Mrs. Wanmacher was acquitted for lack of evidence. Today I learned that a man in Chicago was arraigned for the murder—an old foe of Wanmacher."

"That made the Atlanta papers?"

"No," Margo said, and she was sobbing again. I waited. She cried and cried.

"I waited on Michael at the coffee shop today," she said softly. "I know I'd never have a chance with him anyway, but—he said, 'I never would have dreamed you'd wind up a waitress!'"

"That hurt."

"Not as much as the fact that he was sitting there with his wife and baby."

That would have been enough to send any dreamer to the window, but that wasn't all. Margo continued:

"Michael said he assumed I had heard about Mother's latest bit of celebrity. I almost fainted. 'No.' I said. 'What's that?'"

"'She's been assigned the Wanmacher murder case,' he told me. "They've charged a Chicago mobster, and your mother will be trying the case.'"

THREE

Bill Jacobs, a psychology major at the University of Georgia, lived just down the hall from me. He could hardly believe my story.

"It's not my story," I reminded him. "It's Margo's, and I believe it."

"You do?"

"Shouldn't I?"

"You want the opinion of a friend or a budding psychologist?"

"Whatever."

"As a friend, I'm dubious, but I assume you have no reason not to believe her. I'll bet she's good at spinning a yarn."

"You don't think the suicide attempt was serious?"

"Sure I do, Phil," Bill said, "if she was really doing it in private until you happened along. I don't doubt she's suicidal. I doubt that this bizarre twist—her mother's trying a man for a murder that she herself committed—would be enough to push Margo to the brink."

"Maybe you're right," I said, "but just seeing Michael again wouldn't be quite that devastating either."

"Agreed."

"Then what really set her off?" I asked.

"You don't see it yet, do you?"

"You're the psych major. Let's hear it."

"OK," Bill said. "A man comes between a happily married, or seemingly happily married, man and his wife. The daughter retreats into unreality as her secure world begins to crumble. When she discovers who the other man is, she can see only that he is to blame for her parents' deteriorating marriage. She doesn't suspect her father of also running around on his wife. She doesn't suspect her mother of having become a tramp. She simply feels compelled to rectify the situation, to put things back the way they were. So she shoots the 'other man.' Her mother knows it and uses her knowledge to force Margo out of town, unable to do much else and keep her own secret. So there's a standoff for a few years. But now the case winds up in Mommy's court. Margo figures she can't keep her guilt hidden much longer, so she heads for the window."

"I sure hope you're wrong."

"I s'pose you do, Philip. But you'd better decide before you get in any deeper with her."

"You mean I should be afraid of her?"

"I wouldn't think so," Bill said. "Unless your discovery that she's the murderer would force her to react violently again. Until then, she has no reason to harm you."

"This is crazy," I said. "We're talking about a fragile human being. I'm not buying that she could have committed the murder."

"Then why the guilt? Why a suicide?"

"Is it possible," I asked, "that everything hit her at once and it was simply too much for her? I mean seeing Michael would be traumatic enough, even if he weren't married. Add to that the continuing neglect of her father, her idol. And then the memory of the murder is forced upon her again. She feels unloved, without even the hope of winning her Michael anymore. Like she told me, she had no reason to live, and that was reason enough to die."

"Maybe," Bill said. "Maybe you should be the psychologist."

"No, thanks. Your types are too suspicious."

"Well, I maintain that she's the guilty one, and something else too."

"Which is?"

"You don't want to hear it."

"Of course I do."

"No, really. I'm sorry I got into it."

"I'll bet I know."

"What?" Bill said.

"You don't want to hear it," I said, laughing.

"OK," he said. "You win. I say the religious line you fed her is just going to give her another cover for her guilt. And if she's a murderer, you're gonna wish you'd never used it just to get her away from the window."

"That isn't the only reason I 'fed it to her,'" I objected. "And what if she's telling the truth?"

"Then she's gonna be mighty disappointed when she finds out there's no real value for her in religion."

"If I thought there was no value in it for her, I'd never have brought it up."

"You didn't just hit her with it to keep her from jumping?"

"No," I said, without enough conviction.

"You're not sure, are you?"

"Why don't drop psychology and go into law?" I said.

"Why don't you drop religion and get into reality? If you really believe this stuff, and I'm beginning to fear that you just might, what are you going to tell her next?"

"First of all, I haven't said anything about religion. I'm talking to her about a person."

"I know, I know. Campus Crusade for Christ has made the rounds, and I've heard the whole pitch. It's still religion, and pie in the sky is not going to help this Margo. Murderer or not, she's suicidal, and you'd better have something practical to offer."

I couldn't get Bill's challenge off my mind. Margo had told me that she wasn't ready for my "sermon." I took it to mean she might be soon. She at least had postponed her own death because I promised to tell her of Jesus' love for her. Or had it been just because I seemed to care? I decided I wouldn't mention "religion" to Margo again until she brought it up.

Margo called me late that evening. "I went to work today," she said.

"You're kidding."

"No, I needed something to do, and I didn't want the people at work to think I've quit."

"Why not?"

"Because I haven't. And anyway, I haven't heard your sermon yet."

"I wish you'd quit calling it a sermon."

She ignored me. "If it's as good as you made it sound, maybe I'll be around awhile."

"You weren't ready for it yesterday," I said.

"That was yesterday. I'll be ready tomorrow. I'm going to bed now, but I just wanted to thank you."

I could hardly believe she had gotten up for work after having gone to bed so late. I sure hadn't. I had slept until noon before talking with Bill, and wound up doing a few pencil roughs until Margo called.

It was mid-morning the next day when the phone rang and a woman's voice asked for Mr. Philip Spence. It was a secretary at the art studio where I had applied for a job. I was to meet with Mr. Willoughby for lunch. That sounded good. It wasn't likely he wanted to have lunch with me just to say no to my job application.

"We like your stuff," Mr. Willoughby said over salad. "I wish we could hire you full-time."

I winced. "You wish?"

"I know we interviewed you for the full-time spot, but we're really looking for a beginner—somebody we could pay a modest salary to do cleanup work, keyline, paste up, that sort of thing."

I admitted I didn't relish a full-time job cutting and pasting and that I wouldn't be able to work for that little at this stage in my career.

"We've got something else you might be interested in," he said. He described an account he had recently landed that called for illustrating a series of textbooks. The client wanted cohesiveness and hundreds of small illustrations in a particular style. "I showed him some of the samples you left with me yesterday, and he likes your technique."

"That's good to hear."

"The catch is that he would like to print these books within the year."

"Meaning he needs the illustrations when?"

"He needs two hundred illustrations a month for the next three months. All pen and ink, all basically the same size and format."

"Sounds boring," I said.

"Does fifteen dollars apiece sound boring? That would be nine thousand in three months, or less than three months if you choose to work faster."

"Make it an even ten thousand and I'll start tomorrow." It was a crazy thing to say. I'd never had such an easy and lucrative assignment offer, and here I was risking it for another $1,000.

"OK, the manuscripts are in my car," he said.

I was thrilled with the job, boring though it might be. I could complete eight drawings in three hours each evening and spend my days trying to solicit more business. It was a free-lance artist's dream.

That evening Margo showed up at my apartment. "I'm sorry I didn't call," she said. "I can't go to work anymore; I'm going to quit. I can't handle it." She waved a newspaper as she talked. She hadn't even taken off her coat. She worried me. This was the Margo I had first met, but at mach speed.

"If you've got something to tell me about God, you'd better get on with it," she plunged on, "because I'm not gonna be around here long."

I hadn't said a word. I felt like the center of a merry-go-round, turning as she circled the room. Finally I sat down. Margo didn't. When she paused for a split second I said, as nonchalantly as possible, "I got a great assignment last night."

"Don't you even care, Philip?" she pleaded. "Haven't you been listening?"

"Margo, I've been listening, but you haven't said anything. Yesterday you worked and seemed to have your head on half straight for the first time since I met you. Now you come here unexpectedly and rattle on about doing away with yourself. And I don't even know—"

She cut me off. "I didn't mean suicide. I meant I might be going to Chicago. I can't sit by here and pretend nothing is happening while Mother is in Chicago trying someone else for her own crime. I could never live with myself. I have to go there."

"You mean your mother is actually going through with trying the case?"

Margo unrolled the Atlanta newspaper. A three-inch story announced the trial date a month away in Virginia Franklin's court.

"Margo, do you honestly believe your mother could have murdered Richard Wanmacher and still have the guts to try someone else for it?"

"You think because she's going through with it, that proves her innocence?" she said, incredulous.

"I've heard of scoundrels," I said, "but this would beat everything. How could she sleep?"

"I've wondered that for years," Margo said.

"If you went, would you expose her?"

"No."

"Then why go?"

She had no answer.

"What would you do?" I persisted.

"I'd go to the trial and make Mother uncomfortable. Maybe she would confess."

"A woman who would have the audacity to try a man for a

murder she committed would be so intimidated by your presence that she'd confess? Let's be realistic. Are you sure you don't want to go so *you* can confess?"

It hit her between the eyes. She slumped to the couch. "Is that what you think?" she said, beginning to sob. "Tell me it's not!"

"Margo, all I know is that you're not making any sense. You've got a month before the trial. At least keep your job until then. If and when you feel the need to go to Chicago, it had better be to tell the truth. Otherwise don't go."

Margo sulked through the next three days at work and called me every evening to remind me how hurt she was that I would suspect her. We both watched the newspaper for more information about the upcoming trial.

I had a good start on my illustrating project and hit the sidewalks every morning to drum up more business. I wasn't having much luck, and as it turned out, that would be for the best. The opportunity to talk with Margo about Christ hadn't clearly presented itself, but I knew it would, and that drove me to start praying and digging into my Bible as I hadn't done since high school.

I wasn't getting a lot from my study and prayer that would specifically help Margo, but I felt closer to God than ever, and I prayed almost continually that He would give me something to say just to her. A verse, a word of encouragement, anything. Meanwhile, I gave her every book and article I could find. I was recommending apologists I hadn't even read through yet.

I started going to church again too, but Margo would have nothing to do with it. "Not a chance," was all she'd say. "I'll get my sermon from you when I want it. Anyway, when am I supposed to read all your propaganda?"

One day the morning paper carried the story that the defense attorney had filed a motion for a change of venue, charging that the judge had been a personal friend of the deceased. They had worked in the same district and had been involved in many trials together.

"Mother can't argue with that," Margo said, when I showed her the article. "There's no way she can deny they were colleagues, at least friends professionally."

"Even if this works out the way you think it will, Margo, you've still got problems. The same ones you've had all along. Maybe your mother will be forced to turn the trial over to another judge. It's likely she'll be happy to. But what will change?"

Margo didn't answer and it hit me then that Bill Jacobs might have been right. If Margo herself were guilty, the idea of her mother handling the trial would likely scare her half to death. "Your reaction makes me wonder again if you might be involved in this thing yourself," I said finally.

"You've thought so all along," she said quietly.

"No, frankly, I haven't," I said. "I just don't see how the truth will hurt you, if what you're telling me is the truth."

"Don't you see?" she said. "It won't hurt me; it will hurt Daddy. And that will hurt me. I couldn't do it to him."

"You simply can't keep this to yourself," I said.

"Watch me," she said.

The next day's paper reported that the change of venue motion had been denied when Judge Franklin stated unequivocally that she had never known the deceased outside a courtroom situation.

About three days later Margo received a letter from Frederick T. Wahl, attorney for the defense of Antonio Salerno. It stated that she was to come forth with any information about her mother's social or personal relationship with Richard Wanmacher and/or any information regarding the whereabouts of one Olga Yakovich.

"I had almost forgotten about Olga," Margo told me. "She was our housekeeper for about six months before the murder. They could have learned of her only from Daddy. If I knew where she was, I wouldn't even have to worry about whether or not to tell what I know."

"You think your housekeeper knew and would testify if she were found?"

"Maybe. If I heard all the phone calls, surely Olga did too, and she never did get along with Mother."

"Margo, what if they can't trace Olga? What will you do?"

She didn't answer.

"Hasn't the time come to quit running? If your mother murdered Wanmacher, it's going to come out."

"Then let it. I don't have to be the one to make it happen."

"I think you do, and I think you know you'll never have peace until you do."

"If that's peace, I'll stick with turmoil, thank you."

FOUR

Margo's next message from Defense Attorney Wahl was a simple telegram:

MISS FRANKLIN: HAVE YOU INFORMATION CONCERNING 1) ANYTHING OTHER THAN A PROFESSIONAL RELATIONSHIP BETWEEN MR. RICHARD WANMACHER AND JUDGE VIRGINIA FRANKLIN, OR 2) THE WHEREABOUTS OF MRS. OLGA YAKOVICH? RESPOND SOONEST PLEASE.

"They're serious, Margo," I said. "You can't ignore them."

"Then I'll lie," she said.

"No, you won't."

"And why won't I?"

"Because if you do, I'll assume you've lied to me. Have you?"

"No!"

"Not about anything?"

"No!"

It was obvious that Margo wanted to tell me something, but I kept badgering her. "I haven't lied to you, either," I continued. "I told you I know Someone who loves you, and I do."

"Don't you think I know that?" Margo asked. "All my life I've known there was a God and that He wanted me to do what was right."

A weak "You have?" was all I could say.

"Of course. That's why I haven't slept well for years. I've known all along it was wrong not to tell. For a while it got worse every day. Then it got so six to eight hours would pass sometimes without my even thinking of the murder, but I dreamed of it every night. And anyone who reminded me of Daddy or Mother, or anyone named Richard or Michael would set me off and I'd be good for nothing for days.

"Before Michael showed up at the coffee shop with his wife

I had had a feeling of dread for about week. It was as if God were telling me that something was about to break and I'd have to come forward. Something, I think God, was impressing upon me that I would soon be through running."

"Wasn't that sort of a relief?" I asked.

"I can see why you'd think so. But I considered the options and decided that there was no way I could tell what I knew. It would be too painful for me and for Daddy."

"And it would snap whatever shred of hope you were still clinging to that the three of you would be a happy family again."

Margo turned slowly to face me, as if repeating my words in her mind. Her face contorted into a tear-fighting grimace. Her lips quivered and she blinked furiously. "I guess you're right," she managed, the tears gushing now. She made no attempt to hide her face. It was as if she wanted me to know that I had struck home, and that now I would have to share her grief. I felt strangely privileged as she sat, now wide-eyed, virtually crying to me. I could think of nothing to say.

"You look like you're losing weight," I said finally, feeling absurd.

She didn't react.

"I mean, I thought you said you ate when you were upset."

She wiped her face and shook her head in an act of toleration. "I ate my troubles away up to this point, but now that things are really starting to get hot, I have no appetite."

"Maybe that's good, huh?"

"I don't see how it makes much difference. I'm on a dead-end street anyway. You've got me talked or scared out of killing myself, but I guarantee you I'm not enjoying living either."

"You could if you'd let me tell you about the love God has for you."

"In spite of the mess I'm in I'm s'posed to take consolation in the fact that God loves me?"

"Frankly, I can't identify with a problem as serious as

yours," I admitted. "Mine all seem pretty trivial. But I can tell you, He's never failed me. And I've failed Him often."

"You know," Margo said, "I'd been thinking that God was reaching out to me, but I was running. I thought He was after me because of my secret. When you told me He loved me, it just about blew me away. I'd heard the phrase *God is love,* but I never once thought He could or would love me."

"He does."

"You know, Philip, I don't think anything else you could have said that day would have worked." (I couldn't wait to tell Bill Jacobs.)

"You would have jumped right there in front of me?"

"Absolutely. When you refused to leave, you have no idea how close I came to jumping anyway."

I shuddered. "But you didn't because you liked the idea that God loved you?"

"Not really." Now I was puzzled.

"I think that possibility, along with the fact that you really seemed to care, made the difference."

"Did you really think no one would have missed you?"

"I knew it."

"And what do you think now?"

She smiled faintly, then changed the subject. "What am I going to do about the telegram, Phil?"

"You know what I think you should do."

"If I answer truthfully, will they make me go to Chicago?"

"Likely."

"Since you're badgering me into this, will you go with me if I have to go?"

"Oh, boy."

"That's what I was afraid of. I don't think I can do it on my own."

"I'll tell you what," I said. "You make your own decision about how you're going to answer that telegram. No blaming it on me. Then we'll decide about my going to Chicago with you, if you have to go—but it won't be because I talked you into anything."

"I have to know that you'll go with me before I answer the telegram."

"We don't know how long you'd be there. What would I do about my work?"

"I didn't know free-lance artists worked," she said with a smirk. "And what about that hotshot job you've been bragging about? The one that takes you only a few hours a day to keep up with? Why don't you get ahead and then you can take some time off?"

"I'll think about it," I said. "But we've got to make a deal. I won't even consider it unless you tell all you know in this thing. I'm not going up there with you if you're gonna tell some but not all."

"That one *I'll* have to think about."

I knew I was only a few days away from some serious spiritual talk with Margo, and I searched every Christian book and magazine I had for just the right words. On Sunday the pastor talked about not putting God in a box and expecting Him to do everything the way we think it should be done. I filed it away for future reference. One of the things Margo would surely ask would be how a loving God could allow such a tragedy in her life.

As I was working on textbook illustrations the next night, I tried to imagine myself in Margo's position. She had quite a decision to make, a lot more important than my decision whether or not to go with her to Chicago. I didn't want her to take it for granted, but of course I would go. It would mean working twelve hours a day or more on the illustrations first, but it would be worth it. Very little about Margo irritated me anymore, and I found myself wanting to help her, not just feeling obligated. Besides, I just had to meet Virginia Franklin. She had to be one of a kind.

I made one tactical error with Margo. When she came to me with her decision I nearly blew the whole case. "I want to tell the truth," Margo said. "If you'll stick with me on this, I want to get it done. What's the next step?" I told her to respond to the telegram with a simple yes to the first question, that there was more than a professional relationship between Richard Wanmacher and Virginia Franklin, and a simple no to the question concerning Olga's whereabouts.

"That's not the whole truth, though," she said.

"I know. Don't worry—they'll be back to you for the whole truth."

I was way off. A few days later we read that the lawyers for Salerno had won not just a change of venue, but also got the case thrown out of court for lack of evidence. The prosecution lawyer was astounded at the timing of the decision and admitted that the murder case would probably never be solved. "There are no other suspects," he told newsmen.

Margo and I puzzled over the story and the fact that there had been no follow-up on her telegram. "Maybe there's more on it in the Chicago papers," I said. We drove to the library and dug out the last several issues. What we read made us agree with the prosecutor. The timing was weird. The defense had asked for a few days to bring more evidence on their change of venue petition, but before any of what they found was brought up in court, the case was dismissed.

Slowly it began to make sense to me. "I shouldn't have had you respond only to the defense attorney," I said. "He doesn't care about the relationship between your mother and Wanmacher past its use in getting his client off the hook. A hoodlum's lawyers are going to be hoodlums, right?"

"I'm not following you."

"Figure this. Wahl gets your telegram, goes straight to your mother, shows it to her, and scares the life out of her. Her daughter is about to spill the beans. She makes a fast deal. She'll throw the case out on a technicality if he'll destroy the telegram and tell no one."

"Makes sense."

"Of course it does," I said, clapping and drawing angry stares from two librarians. I felt like Sherlock Holmes.

"But what now?" Margo asked.

"You still willing to tell the truth?"

"If it'll do any good."

"It will if you tell the right people. Don't let me talk you into it, but if you really want to get this off your chest, tell the U.S. attorney for Northern Illinois."

"Why him?"

"He'll hassle Wahl and his associates for not pursuing your telegram. He is the one who must file murder charges against your mother. I never should have expected mob lawyers to be friends of the court."

Margo was stony.

"What's the matter?" I asked.

"File charges against Mother?" she repeated. "Philip, I can't do it. An innocent man has been cleared. Isn't that enough?"

FIVE

I was so certain Margo would call during the night that I slept fitfully, imagining the phone ringing every hour or so. She didn't call. I debated calling her the next day, but I decided to wait.

Some quick figuring told me that I would need 225 hours to complete my 600 sketches. To finish in thirty days would mean an investment of seven and a half hours a day. I didn't think I could maintain a pace of eight sketches every three hours for a whole day, but maybe I could work faster in the morning and average my twenty a day.

I dug out the manuscripts and began logging a basic idea for each drawing along with alternative options for several. Late in the evening I found myself half finished and realized that Margo had not called. I called her.

"I put out a fleece," she told me.

"Sounds awfully biblical for a nonreligious type," I said.

"I'm not totally ignorant of the Bible, you know."

"OK, OK, what was your fleece? More important, what did you decide?"

"I'm going to do whatever I have to do. I can't live with this anymore."

"You're doing the right thing, Margo," I said. "What was your fleece?"

"I decided that I'd believe God wanted me to do it if you called me before I called you."

"That's ridiculous," I said. "You knew I'd call if you didn't call me."

"I didn't know for sure that you'd call, and don't make fun of my fleece. It was sheer torture, wondering if you would get tired of all this and forget me. Anyway, my fleece included a time limit."

"Really? And I called at the very last second, right?"

Margo was silent, hurt. Finally she spoke, "Actually, you had until midnight, if you must know."

"You're convinced now that you should tell all? You're not doing it just for me?"

"No, Philip, but I can't do it without you."

"You know it's going to mean a trip to Chicago."

"Will you go with me?" she asked. "I won't go unless you go with me."

She sounded so desperate. I toyed with needling her about putting conditions on God's will, but she seemed too fragile. "You'll be interested to know that I'm halfway through the planning of my big job, and I've figured a way that I can do the whole thing in thirty days."

"Then you'll do it? You'll go with me if I have to go?"

"Yes, but you'd better know now that there'll be no ifs about it. You inform the right people of what you know, and they'll want you in Chicago—that's all there is to it."

"I'd better do it quickly before I change my mind."

"I thought you were convinced this is what God wants you to do."

"Doesn't God ever change His mind?" Margo asked, seriously.

"Not out of fear, and never about what's right or wrong. Listen, Margo, if I'm going to help you with this, you're going to have to help me get my work done. Let's get some supper and we can talk about it."

I picked up Margo at her apartment, but we didn't go out right away. "I thought we were just going out for a sandwich," she said, reacting to my sportcoat.

"Come on," I said, "don't you know an invitation for a date when you hear one? I distinctly said, 'Let's get some supper and we can talk about it.' That's about as debonair as I'm going to get."

"Well, I'm not going anywhere in a sweater and jeans when you're dressed up," she said.

Margo changed into a pants suit. It was the first time I had seen her in anything but her uniform or grubbies. She looked great, but that was all I wanted to say. She seemed too impressionable.

"I know we're only pretending," she said, as if reading my mind. "But I'm going to enjoy my first 'date' in years."

She did seem to enjoy it too. I exaggerated a lot of chivalrous moves, taking her arm, opening doors, ordering for her, and accusing her of offending all feminists. She laughed each time, and I bowed often. During dinner I raised the subject we had met to discuss.

"Can this wait?" she whined. "You're going to spoil the atmosphere."

I stuck out my lower lip and cocked my head. "Up to you," I said. "But we've got to talk soon."

"I'm off tomorrow," she said. "Let's talk then, and we can keep this evening for just our date."

I eyed her warily but she laughed quickly, assuring me that she was taking it as lightly as I was.

I got to know Margo a bit better that night. More at ease than I had ever seen her, she seemed to come into her own in a world of even mock formality. She knew where to stand and sit and what to say and how to move. She was playing it for all it was worth. Anyone who cared to notice (and few, if any, did) would have thought she was being dated, and she loved it. I didn't mind. I felt benevolent.

She forced lightness into the conversation at every point. The heaviest we got was when she admitted that her favorite pastime was no longer reading. "It's television," she said flatly. "When I'm not working or sleeping, I'm watching. I know it's garbage, but I am literally hooked. I hate to miss anything. Sometimes I fall asleep watching and the test pattern is humming when I get up for work.

"There are lots of books and magazines I'd love to read, but I buy them and bring them home and they sit unopened, or quickly scanned, while I watch TV. It's a drag."

"That *does* sound like a drag," I said. "Let's talk about it tomorrow. Can you pass up some television to come over and help me finish my preliminary stuff? This isn't going to be easy, working all day every day—"

"But you'll do it for me, right?" she interrupted.

I didn't smile. It was true, I would do it for her, and I didn't want her to take it lightly. It was going to be an unbelievable job, and I was going to ask her to help me a lot. I wasn't going to feel guilty about it, either.

"I don't give up my favorite programs for even a good book, and you want me to give them up for you?" Her eyes were dancing.

"You'll be giving them up often if you help me as much as I need you to during the next month," I said.

She was still smiling, but I wasn't. "Oh, Philip," she said. "You know I will."

Realizing how stern I looked, I exaggerated my frown and growled, "Good, see that you do." Margo laughed, and I took her home.

At her door I flipped on a British accent. "Such a lovely evening, m'dear," I said. "We must do it again soon." Kissing her hand was as much pretending as I wanted to do. I turned on my heel and headed for the stairs.

"When?" she called after me.

"Give me until about three to finish my planning."

"OK," she said, "I'll see you then."

I got home at about 11:00, but I wasn't tired. I had a lot of work to do in the morning, but I didn't feel like going to bed. I didn't feel like doing anything. I sat staring for about an hour and fell asleep on the couch. In the morning, as I finished listing sketch ideas from the manuscripts, my mind kept drifting to the night before and how unproductive it had been. I worried that Margo might have made too much of it, and what I would do if she had. I decided to be a bit cool to her for a while so she wouldn't get any ideas. *Don't flatter yourself,* my conscience chastised.

I finished my preliminaries and had been napping for an

hour when Margo arrived. "How did you know I hadn't eaten?" I asked.

"Just guessed," she said, opening a dish of home-cooked chicken.

"I want to be serious for a minute, Philip," she said as we ate. "I've been goofing around, but I really do want to know what it's going to take to free you to go to Chicago with me and what I can do to help."

"I'm glad you want to be serious," I said, "because it's not going to be easy.

"First we have to give you a reason to go to Chicago. I've dug out the name of the U.S. attorney for the Northern Illinois district. He's James A. Hanlon."

"What do I tell him? And how?"

I advised Margo to tell Hanlon in a simple, handwritten note that her information, probably incriminating her own mother, Judge Virginia Franklin, had apparently been used to clear Antonio Salerno, but had not been pursued beyond that. "While it makes sense that my mother would not favor pursuing it," Margo wrote, "doesn't it seem that Attorney Frederick Wahl, as a friend of the court, would have checked into it further? I am ready to tell what I know. Are you interested?"

Margo and I went to the post office together and sent the letter with every precaution possible. It was air mail, special delivery, marked *personal, important,* and *confidential,* was insured, and a return receipt was requested. Once the letter was on its way, Margo seemed distant. "If he doesn't do any more with it than Wahl did, I'm going to forget it," she said. "I don't know if I can talk myself into this again."

On the way back to my apartment, I told Margo how many hours a day I figured it would take to do all my work in thirty days.

"Wow," she whispered.

"And I'll need help. But I can do it," I said. "How much money do you have?"

"Why?"

"You're going to have to trust me, Margo. Even if I get this work done, I likely won't be paid for about six weeks. The client has to like it and pay the studio, and the studio has to pay me. That takes time. I have only a few hundred dollars, and I'm going to have to leave that here for rent. Who knows how long we'll be in Chicago?"

"I've got about six hundred dollars."

"Oh, that's be more than enough. We'll use that to get to Chicago and to exist on until my money comes. Then I'll pay you back and still have enough to live on for several months, if necessary."

"I hope it's not necessary," Margo said.

"So do I."

"But my providing money isn't going to keep me from my TV. What else do you want me to do?"

"I want lots of little things done," I said. "I hate to ask, but it's the only way we're going to pull this thing off."

"Just name it, Philip."

"OK. If I'm going to be sketching for nearly eight hours a day, I'm going to have little time for anything else. Can you bring me food after work?"

"Didn't I prove it?"

"Yeah, and it was good."

"What else?"

"I may need errands run. Mail, supplies, sketches delivered."

"Sorry, my social calendar is full this month."

I blinked.

"Seriously, Philip, this will be fun. What else do I have to do? I leave that stinking restaurant every evening and sit home eating and watching TV. This will be the best time I've had in months—years."

"Don't get carried away. I thought you'd feel like a slave."

"No way, especially not when I think of why I'm doing it."

"Just to help your best friend, Phil, right?"

"No, because my best friend, Phil, is helping me."

"I have two other conditions, Margo."

"Oh?"

"First is that we do not discuss what's going to happen in Chicago until we're on our way there. There's no way I can concentrate on my work if we try to hammer out strategy during the day."

"OK."

"The other condition is that I get to talk to you about God during our trip to Chicago."

Margo was fidgeting. "Why is this making me nervous?" she asked.

"Is it a deal?"

"I guess. But can't we talk about Mother and what I'm going to do in Chicago before we talk about God?"

"If we start talking about that, there'll be no time to talk about anything else. Anyway, what we both get out of our discussion about God may help determine what you'll do in Chicago."

"What are you hoping, Philip?"

"That's a loaded question."

"Really, what are you hoping will happen?"

"You really want to know?"

"Yeah."

"I'm hoping that you'll realize how much God loves you, and that it will make you want to receive His love gift. After that I just hope you'll see how righteous God is and how He will honor you for doing what's right."

"Which means what?"

"Exposing the entire truth in Chicago."

"For you that sounds neat and complete and the only thing to do, doesn't it?"

"Yup."

"How do you think it sounds to me?"

She caught me off guard. It had been easy to say what I would do. But what if it really were me? "Uh . . ."

"It sounds like a nightmare," she said.

"Which is what you've been living for years, right?"

Margo nodded.

"Are you still game?" I asked.

"Do I have a choice?"

I began sketching at eight o'clock the next morning and was still going strong when Margo arrived ten hours later. "I'm already ahead of schedule," I told her.

"And what have you eaten?"

"I've been gnawing on pretzel sticks and sipping Coke all day," I said. "What've you got?"

"Something you can eat while you're working," she said.

"Good, what?"

"Pretzel sticks and Coke."

"Oh, no—"

"No, really I brought something from the restaurant. It has to be heated."

I kept sketching while Margo talked. It slowed me down a bit, but I was getting tired anyway, and it sure was a change of pace from ten hours in a quiet apartment.

"When I stopped home to change, my TV stared at me forlornly," she said.

"Forlornly?" I mocked. She set the hot meal before me, and I continued to work as I ate. She looked at the sketches and I looked at her. Her features were soft, her eyes dramatic. I didn't say anything.

"I like them," she said, "I s'pose I'd like them more if I knew their significance."

I showed her the manuscripts for the books and my notations for the required sketches. She was fascinated.

"You know, I never saw any of your work before," she said.

"I guess that's right, come to think of it," I said. "Sorry."

"So am I. I'm not a professional, but in my opinion you're exceptionally good."

"That makes you a professional," I teased.

"How come you don't hang any of your work around the apartment?"

"Never thought of it, I guess. Anyway, I sell most everything I do."

"There's something sad about that," Margo said.

"What?"

"I don't know," she said.

Margo ran the first several sketches over to the art studio and mailed some letters for me. She returned just in time to answer the phone. I winced. "What if it's my mother?" I said as she picked up the receiver. It wasn't.

"It's the art studio."

"Yes, sir." I answered.

"Was that your wife?" Mr. Willoughby asked.

"No, just a friend," I said, knowing how it sounded.

"Uh-huh," he said. "Listen, Phil, I just wanted to tell you what I thought of the first sketches."

"You've seen them already?"

"Yeah. I just got back from supper. I can't speak for the client, but I think we're smack on the right track and I wanted to encourage you."

"That's good to hear. I'll be eager to know what the client thinks."

"Me too. I'll let you know as soon as I can. Probably in a few days."

SIX

Earl Haymeyer looked too young, short, and thin to be a detective, but his credentials said he was a special investigator for the office of United States Attorney James A. Hanlon. Haymeyer wore a suit and carried an attaché, but he also carried a snub-nosed .38 and spoke quickly.

"My boss was a personal friend of Richard Wanmacher and is a bitter enemy of both Wahl and Salerno. He has always suspected some sort of an affair between Judge Franklin and Mr. Wanmacher, but he never knew anything for sure. He spent years trying to nail someone for the murder and was very suspicious of Judge Franklin when the case against Salerno was tossed out. Then he got the letter from your girlfriend."

"She's not my girlfriend," I said. "Just a friend."

"We're not amateurs, Mr. Spence. When my boss couldn't reach your girlfriend by phone, we sent a telegram."

He pulled a copy from his brief case. "MISS FRANKLIN: HAVE BEEN UNABLE TO REACH YOU BY PHONE. CALL IMMEDIATELY. JAMES A. HANLON."

"When she still didn't call, I was assigned to locate her. I traced her phone number to her apartment complex and left a message at the office there. They told me where she worked."

"You could have reached her at her place late at night," I said.

"Or here at your place any other time, right?"

"Well, yeah. Y'see, I—"

"I know, Mr. Spence. I was just getting worried about her."

"You were worried? Why?"

"Because I've also been keeping a tail on Mr. Salerno."

All I could think of was that he would be no match for the

notorious hit man, who had been charged with murder nine times but never convicted. Haymeyer saw it in my eyes.

"We're not amateurs, Mr. Spence," he repeated. "Mr. Hanlon and I wondered why Judge Franklin would make a deal with a hit man and his lawyer until your girlfriend's letter arrived. Then it made sense, especially when my sources showed Salerno arranging a trip to Atlanta under a phony name. You see why we wanted to get ahold of Margo quickly?"

"Tell me."

Haymeyer was impatient. "Margo's letter tells us that her info, implicating her mother, was ignored by Wahl. But Salerno is cleared and heads for Atlanta. Adding up?"

It was, but I continued to look puzzled. I wanted to hear it all.

"I think old lady Franklin contracted to have her daughter taken out of the picture."

"You're kidding," I said, knowing immediately how it sounded. Haymeyer pursed his lips, but left the 'we're-not-amateurs' line unrepeated.

"How did you find me?" I asked.

"We found Margo first," he said. "When Salerno actually started heading south by car, I flew down here and met Margo at the restaurant. She's in a motel room now, but she told me all about you, and that she won't go to Chicago or say any more unless you're with her."

"Did she say I was her boyfriend?" I asked.

"She said the same thing you've been saying," Haymeyer said. "But you're *not* her lawyer, and we're—"

"Not amateurs," I cut him off. We both smiled.

"I'll take you to her," he said.

"How do I know you're really working for Hanlon?" I asked.

"I thought you'd never ask." He produced the original of the letter Margo had sent Hanlon. "You don't suppose I found this in the garbage, do you?"

I talked Haymeyer into letting me drop off the rest of my completed sketches at the art studio, and in the process I got more encouragement from Mr. Willoughby. He said the client was thrilled but was concerned about how fast I was working.

"What does he care, as long as the stuff is good?"

"He hasn't complained about the artwork, Philip. He just wants you to know that you're a couple of months ahead and that you can slow up if you wish."

"I might just do that. Could he pay you so you can pay me for what's done so far?"

"No problem."

On the way to the motel, Haymeyer showed me several photographs of Salerno. "We figure it won't take Salerno long to track down Margo once he gets here, which should be sometime late tonight."

"Won't he have to learn her schedule or something before he tries anything?"

"Very good, kid. You've been watching TV, haven't you? Tomorrow's Sunday. Does Margo work on Sunday?"

"Usually, but not tomorrow."

"Salerno will have to figure that out. He'll probably show up at the restaurant and go to her apartment when he realizes that she's off work. If she's not there he may wait, or he might start asking questions that lead him to your place."

"Meanwhile we're jetting off to Chicago, right?"

"Not quite."

"Oh?"

"What you don't realize, kid, is that we have several objectives."

"We?"

"The U.S. attorney's office. First is the safety of Miss Franklin, not to mention you."

"Please mention me."

"Second is to solve the Wanmacher murder case, which my boss, not to mention the public, wants very much to see."

"Is there a third?"

"Yeah, and that's why we're not jetting off to Chicago while Salerno is looking to blow Margo's head off."

"I guess I'm ready for number three."

"You sure, kid?"

"Why do you call me kid? You can't be much older than I am."

"So it makes me feel older; am I forgiven?"

"What's your third objective?"

"To nail Salerno. In the act."

"In the act?"

"Of murdering Margo."

It hadn't dawned on me until that instant that I was in over my head. Talking Margo out of killing herself had been the most traumatic experience in my life. Everything since then had seemed slow motion, even a visit from a government detective who told me Margo was being stalked by a mob hit man. But Margo as live bait?

"You can't really let her stay in Atlanta while he looks for her, can you?"

"We can and we will. I have some associates on the way right now. Our plan is to let Salerno have a good look at Margo and her schedule. We'll be watching her and him all the time, and I hope we'll set him up."

"You hope?"

"Frankly, despite his eluding conviction in nine previous arrests, and despite the fact that we believe he's guilty of twice as many successful hits, I think we've got a real chance here."

"Why?"

"He's limited by his *modus operandi.*"

"Which is?"

"Clean and messy at the same time. Sawed-off shotgun."

I was speechless. Was this real?

Haymeyer continued. "Salerno is good, maybe the best, with a sawed-off. But this is not the kind of a hit that can be pulled off in public. And it's not Salerno's style to come in shooting. If it was, he'd have been locked up years ago.

"No, he's very cool and crafty. He lies low, is seldom noticed, even when asking someone's whereabouts."

"Why is that?"

"He uses simple disguises. He's very ordinary anyway. He doesn't have the sinister look that people expect after seeing too many cops and robbers on TV. His average build and appearance lend themselves to disguise and anonymity."

"When and how does he make his, uh, hits?"

"He takes his time. He makes a lot of money, and he makes sure. My guess is that he'll watch Margo for four or five days until he is sure of the one place he can nail her without the chance of anyone interfering."

"I think I'd rather see her hustled off to Chicago."

"Then what would we have? A hit man on the loose, still looking for her—and for you, for that matter. If he follows her, it's going to lead to you, you know."

All I could think of was that neither Bill Jacobs nor my parents would ever believe this.

"There's something else," Haymeyer said. "If we don't get Salerno, who's going to give us what we need to put away old lady Franklin?"

"Margo."

"I've heard Margo's story. It's heavy, but it'll never stand up without Salerno admitting that he was paid by the judge to kill Margo."

"Did Margo tell you about Olga?"

"We've been looking for Olga ever since Wahl and his boys stumbled onto her name during the Salerno pretrial."

"How did they get onto her?"

"Through Mr. Franklin is all we can figure."

"That doesn't sound like something he'd say, based on what Margo told me," I said.

"We figure it was an innocent comment he made in response to questions about anyone who had contact with Mrs. Franklin at the time of the murder. Wahl was really pushing Judge Franklin at this point, and he wanted to discover and use any and every name that might fluster her into throwing out the case."

"Margo's name was the one that did it, though, right?"

"It appears that way. We've talked to Mr. Franklin, and he's convinced not only that Mrs. Franklin can in no way be suspected, but also that she never was unfaithful to him. I think the judge figures he's not worth worrying about, or she'd have sent Salerno after *him*."

"She must not be worried about Olga either, then?"

"I'm not so sure," Haymeyer said. "Like I said, we haven't been able to locate her. I'd hate to think she's already been eliminated."

"What a nice way to say it," I said.

Margo looked like a scared puppy. Haymeyer looked nonplussed that we didn't embrace.

"Where could Olga be, Margo?" I said.

"I have no idea," she said. "I never really knew her, and I didn't hear from her after she quit."

"She quit?" Haymeyer said, taking off his top coat and shoes and stretching out on one of the beds.

"Yes, just after the murder. I always figured she knew about Mother and Richard."

Haymeyer rolled over quickly and grabbed the telephone. He placed a person-to-person call to Hanlon in Chicago. "Jim, Earl. I've got Margo and her boyfriend here, and we're going to try to flush out Salerno. . . . Yes, I've already requested Barnes and Warren, if that's OK. . . . Good. Listen, Jim, is there someone there who can work full time in tracking down this Olga what's-her-name?"

"Yakovich," Margo offered.

Haymeyer wheeled around. "Right, Yakovich. I think she might be key in this, Jim. If anything goes wrong with

Salerno—" Haymeyer paused, and I saw the fear in Margo's eyes. "Oh, no, I don't mean that," Haymeyer was saying. "I mean if he won't talk once we get him. We'll get him."

He sounded so certain.

That evening detectives Jim Barnes and Bob Warren arrived at the Atlanta airport and called Haymeyer at his motel room. They were each instructed to rent a car and to meet us at the Omni, Atlanta's professional sports complex. "The Hawks don't generally draw as many fans now that they are playing without their old stars," Haymeyer told his two men. "But with the Seventy-sixers visiting tonight, we'll be unnoticed in the crowd."

"It's just like a date," Haymeyer told Margo and me. "You go to the game in Philip's car. It's unlikely Salerno will have the faintest idea where to find you yet, but we'll not appear to be together anyway. We three will sit behind you. When we sit down, you two lean back as if bored with the game. We will sit forward and talk with each other so you can hear. You'll get the whole picture, but don't look at us, and don't say anything to us. My guess is that Salerno is in Atlanta by now, and he'll be following every lead to get at Margo. He's no amateur either."

Haymeyer dropped us off at my apartment, where we got in my car and headed for the Omni. We arrived early and were fascinated by the crowd and the game, but we found it hard to talk. "Where's God now?" Margo asked.

"Only you could make that sound original," I said.

I tried not to look around but found myself constantly watching for Haymeyer. When he arrived I almost didn't recognize him. He was wearing a Hawks hat and was carrying a box of popcorn. We leaned back, still looking straight ahead, and he leaned forward. "Look all around the stadium," he said quietly, "and you'll see Bob Warren in the green pullover, heading this way."

Margo looked one way and I looked the other, and we both eventually spotted Warren. He too had popcorn and a Hawks hat, but he looked out of place—older, gruffer, and tackier than Haymeyer.

"Jim Barnes is coming from the other way," Haymeyer said. We caught ourselves looking too quickly. Tall, thin, and blond, Barnes looked like a country gentleman out for a night of fun with his buddies. He was Warren's age.

The three detectives were boisterous about the game and the bets and the beer, but during the time-outs and between quarters they all leaned forward, elbows on knees, and chatted seriously in low tones, just loud enough for Margo and me to hear. Occasionally, though they were talking seriously, one would smack the other on the back or lean back and laugh uproariously, spilling something.

"Margo," Haymeyer said, "I'm going to talk about your schedule for the next few days. If you don't understand something, just turn and say something about the game to Phil and I'll repeat it. If you miss something altogether, we can talk about it later. If you understand, just shake your head as if to rearrange your hair." Margo shook her head and I turned to look. Her hair was beautiful. She was scared. So was I. I took her hand.

"That looks good, Philip. Just like a date. Now after the game you just take her to her place and then go home." I almost turned around. With Salerno in town I was to leave her alone in her apartment?

Haymeyer leaned back in his seat and called for a vendor. After buying an ice-cream bar he leaned forward to unwrap it. "Will you leave her safety to us?" he hissed. "Bob has already rented an apartment on her floor and will be there before you are. She will be under constant watch. It's unlikely that Salerno will show up there tonight anyway. Jim has rented a place in your building, Philip, though not on your floor. He'll be close whenever Margo is there, but there's no need for him to be on your floor otherwise. Salerno won't want you without Margo.

"Jim, I want each of us to visit the restaurant once in the

next three days. None of us will be there more than once, in case Salerno is watching and notices a pattern. Margo, if you have a message for us, write it out and give it to us with our bill. The key is for you to maintain your usual routine. Any time, remember, *any time* you find yourself alone, walk very quickly and do not linger. Keep moving. The key is to make Salerno think that the only place he has a chance to get you is in your apartment, either while you're asleep or watching television."

Margo turned to look at me. "You don't understand something?" Haymeyer asked. I wrote a question on my program and dropped it beneath the seat. Barnes picked it up and read the question while passing it back to me. "Thanks," I said.

Barnes said to Haymeyer, "He'd rather the trap be laid at his apartment so Margo won't be alone."

I could tell from the sound of Barnes's voice that he was as annoyed as Haymeyer, who leaned almost to my ear and said sternly, "Philip, we know what we are doing. Leave it to us. There is no way we'll let Salerno get into Margo's apartment while she is there. If he tries, we'll nail him before he gets through the door. What we want is for him to get into the apartment when we have a dummy there. If he puts a load of buckshot through a dummy, we have a strong case. If he tries to get in before we think he will, and Margo is there instead of a dummy, we'll take him immediately." I settled back, nodding.

"There's something none of us should forget," Warren said. "We don't know Salerno is even aware of Margo. We don't know that's why he's here, or even that Mrs. Franklin let him off because of Margo's message to Wahl. We're going to approach the case as if he's here to get her, but we're only guessing. Let's not forget that."

Everyone nodded and Warren clapped Haymeyer on the back. "Gotta get goin'!" he said, and reached across to shake Barnes's hand.

"See ya," Barnes said.

Twenty minutes later the 76ers were sure of victory and many fans were leaving. "Stay until you see us leave," Haymeyer said. "Give us about a ten-minute lead. I'm staying at the motel, and Barnes will be at your place by the time you get there, Philip. He'll nod to you in the hall when you get to your apartment. If he doesn't, call me immediately."

I was tingling with excitement and fear on the way to Margo's apartment.

"It's ironic," she said with a shiver, "not two weeks ago I wanted to kill myself. Now someone is going to try to do it for me."

"He won't succeed, though," I said, trying to sound brave. "These guys, Haymeyer and his boys, are too good." Margo said nothing. "Have you read those articles I gave you?" I asked.

"Yes, but I'm not thinking about them right now," Margo said. "If you had a Bible, I might read that." I leaned across her and popped open the glove compartment. I gave her a *Living New Testament.* "It's easy to read," I said.

"And that's what I need, right?" she said.

I blushed. "I mean it's easier to understand. At least for me."

"You're not as well read as I am, remember," she said, sounding chippy.

"What's wrong, Margo?"

"Oh, nothing," she said. "It's just that I'm about to have my head blown off, and my only friend in the world thinks he's got an edge on brains because he's a man."

"Now I'm a chauvinist?" I said. "I do think I have an edge on reality, though; I haven't thought about suicide."

"Oh, that helped," she said.

"I'm sorry. I didn't mean it to come out like that."

"It's OK, Philip, I deserved it. It's just that Haymeyer never asked if I wanted to cooperate in this scheme. I haven't even had time to think about it."

"There isn't time," I said.

"Time isn't the point, Philip."

"What is the point?"

"That I feel nothing toward the man who is hunting me down. I don't even feel anything toward the woman who's paying him to do it."

"You don't?"

"No, and that's the problem. I should hate her, but all I can do is wonder why my own mother would want me killed."

"You know why."

"Sure I know the pragmatic reasons, but how did it come to this? Is she so afraid for her own neck that she would kill her daughter? She threw away her marriage and family for what? A man? What was so special about Richard Wanmacher that she would sacrifice her family for him and then hate him to the point that she would kill him?"

"She did the same for you. She loved you and now she hates you."

"Oh, it hurts to hear those words from anyone but me."

"I know, and I'm sorry."

"You may be sorry, but no, Philip, you don't know. How could you know?"

Margo was right. It choked me up to think of my own mother. Overprotective, possessive, eccentric perhaps. Old-fashioned. Devout. I would never belittle her again, not even to myself. What I would give for my mother! And what I would give if Margo could have had a mother like mine.

"Philip, I am about to risk my life so a murderer my mother hired can be trapped into implicating her. Yet I feel no anger. I just feel alone, abandoned."

"You have God."

"I do, but not in the way you think."

"I don't follow."

"No, you don't, Philip. I don't say this to put you down, please believe that, but I think you're too naive to see how I have God when I have no one else. In all that you've shown me and told me and given to me to read about God, I've learned more about Him than I think you know."

I was shocked. What could she have learned about God that I hadn't known?

"You've been trying to reach me with intellectual arguments," she continued. "You thought I would need every barrier and doubt eradicated. You've given me evidence and reason and verses and everything else. It has all been reassuring, but that's not why I asked Jesus to be my Christ."

"You did? When?"

"When is irrelevant now, Philip."

"But why didn't you tell me? Didn't you think I'd want to know?"

"I knew you'd want to know, but I wasn't sure why. Was it because you wanted to tell your Sunday school class or pastor or your friends or your parents? Was I a trophy?"

"You don't really think that, do you, Margo?"

"I don't know. I know I was more than a trophy for you at first, when you approached me with God as an alternative to death. That is beautiful, because that's what I have discovered Him to be. The antithesis of death."

Margo sounded so cool and calculated. Perhaps I had been out of my league intellectually, in spite of my subconscious chauvinism. It seemed that she was begrudging, almost attacking the fact that she had found Christ and was being careful not to credit me in any way.

"It's not that I'm ungrateful, Philip. And if it weren't for what I'm going through, I'm sure I wouldn't be picking you apart. It's just that you have communicated something to me that you didn't mean to communicate, and that very thing was what led me to Christ."

I was almost irritated. "What in the world was it?"

"It's so simple," Margo said. "In all the things you said and gave me to read, it wasn't the arguments that made the difference. It wasn't anything but the fact that I had God in you."

"Careful."

"No, I won't be careful. I'm not trying to flatter you, don't you see? Good grief, God uses you in spite of yourself. Your faith and your Christianity—and even your God is so small to you that you limit Him."

She was rambling on nervously, watching each street sign as we neared her place, probably hoping that we wouldn't arrive too soon. Haymeyer had cautioned me not to sit in the car and talk, and not to drive around the block in front of her place. He wanted Salerno, if he was watching, to think everything was normal.

"You see, Philip, God used you in the most simple and profound way possible. He loved me and cared about me through you. When I was immature and half insane with fear and guilt, He somehow allowed you to cope even though you really couldn't care and probably couldn't have coped."

I was hurt, and it showed.

"Don't misunderstand, Philip. You *are* misunderstanding. I can tell. That's my whole point. You thought you were God's mouthpiece. You weren't. If I had listened to your arguments and had taken seriously all of what your fundamentalist theologians call—what is it, apologetics?—I could have debated this thing for years. I likely would not have made the decision that I did."

"I had nothing to do with it, then?"

"Your nervousness is limiting your logic now too, Philip. You had everything to do with it, because in all of this, the only place I saw God was in you. Hearing you, knowing you, reading your literature only proved to me what an unlikely candidate you were to be used of God. When you first mentioned to me that God loved me it nearly blew me away—"

"Bad choice of words."

She ignored my grim humor. "But what you said was a shred of hope. I wanted evidence that God loved me, as you said He did."

"I tried to give you evidence."

"And all I needed was to see that you cared. Didn't you ever ask yourself why you were involved?"

"As a matter of fact, yes."

"Then you should be able to see it. There was no reason for you to care. Sure, you're a nice guy and all, but your arguments and attempts at convincing me were just evidence that the real you was just trying to do the right thing. It was Christ in you that convinced me."

"I don't know how to feel, Margo. Are you chastising me?"

"No. In fact, I don't think I would tell you to change in any way, except maybe to realize what's important and what isn't. In a way, you had to be the way you were for the chemistry to be just right. Had I not seen your humanity in all your efforts to convince me of God's love, I'd have never seen the contrast in the way God used you in spite of yourself. It had to be the way it was."

"If my arguments were all so futile, why didn't you say so?"

"I guess because there was something strange going on. You were loving me, almost, without knowing it. Not the romantic kind of love, but with God's love. I looked to you for unconditional love, the kind you talked about, and the kind I read about. God loved me unconditionally through you, and you hardly knew it."

I had nothing to say. For sure, I had underestimated Margo's mind. "You have unusual insight," I said finally. "I've always heard that when you're trying to win someone to Christ you should just let God use you and trust His Spirit to do the work."

"That's what happened, Philip. Every time I tried to pray, it seemed as if God were telling me not to listen to you so much as to watch you love me. It was as if He were saying, 'This is how I love you. Through Philip.'"

"That's almost scary, and sort of embarrassing and humbling too."

"Philip, I love you in Jesus. I can say that because I know

you love me in Him. I love you because you loved me first. That's why we love Christ, according to one of those articles you gave me."

"Then you did get something from them?"

"You're missing my point, Philip," she said, patiently. "I got a lot from them. Mostly I learned what to look for in you. I saw it, in spite of you."

"I don't know whether to feel thrilled or insulted."

"Feel used. God used you. I don't understand why you haven't seen this in your Bible reading. Isn't that what the Bible is all about?"

"Yes, but I guess when it becomes old to a person, he misses the real point—the living part of it."

"You didn't miss it, Philip. You just hit it without knowing it."

"One of my problems is the problem of every Christian I know: the discipline of daily Bible reading."

"Why do you have a problem if you believe it's God's Word?"

"If I knew the answer to that one, I could save a lot of people a lot of grief."

"No, really, Philip. Do you realize how that sounds? You tell me you believe this book is the Word of God. I couldn't hope for anything better than to have the Word of God in a book. Then you tell me that the people who believe this are the ones who have the trouble reading it every day. Why?"

"I don't know, Margo. I do know that every time I force myself to read and study, I am thrilled. God gives me something special. If it's not a specific answer to a need of the day, it might just be some encouragement in the way a psalm is worded or in the way a writer has praised God. Still, it's a struggle to read it faithfully."

"I don't know whether I'll ever understand why a person has to force himself to read something he loves," Margo said. "All I want to do is read the Bible. Will I lose that desire?"

"You might. You're going through what many people call the 'first love of Christ.' I think it's even called that in the New Testament."

"It's all so clinical. I hope I don't fit into some prescribed pattern. I'm going to read the Bible tonight. If Antonio Salerno wants to blow me away tonight, I'll die reading the Bible."

"You've become an amazingly mature Christian overnight," I said, only half joking.

"I'm not saying I'm not scared. I'm still puzzled about a lot of things too. Somehow, I am convinced of the unconditional love and the ultimate wisdom of God. If a person who goes through what I've been through can say that, you know only God has convinced me of it."

"That's for sure, Margo. That's what I figured would be my biggest hurdle: convincing you that God was in this whole mess."

"There you go. Your biggest hurdle? You were going to convince me of it? Never. Only God could do it, and not with words."

We both spotted Bob Warren in the lobby, sitting in a stuffed chair and smoking idly. Our eyes met briefly. Margo left me at her door and went in with the *Living New Testament* tucked under her arm. When I returned to my apartment, I saw no trace of Jim Barnes—not in the parking lot, not in the lobby, not on the elevator, not in the hall. I walked slowly, trying to be totally alert. I spent a long time unlocking my door and began to panic when I still didn't see him.

"Call me immediately," had been Haymeyer's instruction.

"Room three thirty-three please," I said. His phone rang six times.

"There seems to be no answer, sir."

"Ring again, please. I know he's there."

She rang the room again, eight times. "I'm sorry, sir."

SEVEN

I imagined the worst and kept calling Haymeyer's number. The desk clerk finally offered to leave the message light on in his room and was obviously relieved to have me off her back. Margo's line was busy, so with nothing to do but worry, I took a walk in the building, hoping to see Barnes.

I passed two medium-sized men about five minutes apart, certain each time that I had discovered the hit man Salerno. I hadn't, of course, but I would have suspected a poodle at that point.

The phone was ringing when I got back to my apartment, but I didn't get to it in time. I called Haymeyer.

"No, sir. Now, please, I said I'd have him call!" the operator snapped.

I called Margo. Still busy. I slammed the receiver down. The phone rang.

"What have you been doing?" Haymeyer demanded. "For a half hour your line is busy, and then I get no answer until now."

"I've been trying to reach you, Earl," I said. "Barnes is not here and Margo's line is busy and—"

"I know all that. I'm calling from Margo's. Meet me at the drugstore on your corner in half an hour, and I'll fill you in. Let's not talk by phone."

"What's up? Is Margo all right?"

"Let's not talk by phone," Haymeyer said sternly, and he hung up.

"Yes, Margo is fine," Haymeyer said at the drugstore as we scanned magazines. "It's just that her mother called, and Margo thought we should know. She called Warren and he called Barnes when I couldn't be reached."

"Why couldn't you be reached?"

"I had a message to call Chicago and didn't want to call from my room. I was out making the call when they were trying to reach me. When I got back and didn't get an answer at Barnes's room, I headed for Margo's."

"Why couldn't you call Chicago from your room?"

"Salerno may not be alone here. It's possible our phones are tapped."

"Even mine?"

"Most likely yours. I'm still hopeful Salerno is not aware that we're here in Atlanta, but you can bet he's aware of you. If he finds out we're here, it may scare him off."

"That would be nice."

"No, it wouldn't. I think the phone call from Judge Franklin tonight may play right into our hands."

"What was it all about? Margo says Mrs. Franklin rarely calls and never just for chitchat."

"It wasn't chitchat, Philip. It was a setup. First of all, she wasn't calling from home. Margo heard street noises. That's smart."

"Why?"

"Because if she is working with Salerno and wants Margo snuffed, it would look bad to have a call to Atlanta on her bill the day before. She underestimated Margo, though. It was stupid to call from a pay phone and expect Margo to think she was calling from home.

"Mrs. Franklin said she was passing along a message from Margo's father, whom she claimed to have seen recently. He wanted her to be sure to be at home tomorrow evening at nine so he could find her there when he calls, she said."

"You sure it's a setup?" I asked.

"Yup. We made sure Margo's phone was not bugged and had her call her father. Luckily she caught him at his apartment, and he seemed pleased to hear from her. She made no mention of the message from Mrs. Franklin, and neither did he."

"Earl," I said, "what are the odds that Mr. Franklin wouldn't mention the coincidence of Margo calling the night before he planned to? Or that he wouldn't ask if she'd gotten a message from her mother?"

"The odds are he would, Philip. You're catching on."

"What do you suppose is happening?"

"It's pretty transparent. Judge Franklin is so intent on Salerno completing the job that she's helping out. Do you suppose Salerno has any idea where Margo might be tomorrow night?"

"By the phone in her apartment."

"Right."

"What are you going to do?"

"Watch Salerno, and use a dummy."

"You've spotted Salerno?"

"Warren thinks he has."

"He *thinks?*"

"That's enough for me, Philip. We don't take chances when it comes to safeguarding a witness."

"That's good to hear. What about a witness's friend?"

Haymeyer loved the idea that Margo and I were going to church the next morning. He said he and Barnes would meet us there while Warren stayed at Margo's building to keep an eye on Salerno. "What do people wear to church in this town?" he wanted to know.

"Same as everywhere," I said. "Dress up, and carry a Bible or you will stand out as a stranger."

"I want to look like anything but a stranger," he said. "I'll pass along any more info when I greet you after Mass."

"It's a *service* in this church," I said.

"OK, when I greet you after the service. They do greet each other after the service, right?"

I picked up Margo the next morning and saw her in pastel for the first time.

"It's a step," she said. "I'm not sure I'm really ready for light colors, but I feel like I am."

"I think you are," I said, staring too long.

Margo admitted that she had hardly slept but had read until about 4:00 A.M. "I did feel a little more secure knowing that Mr. Warren was in the building, but every noise froze me to the bed. I prayed a lot."

Barnes and Haymeyer were a sight, each carrying Gideon Bibles from Earl's motel. They shook hands with us like old friends and smiled as they talked. Jim told us that the Atlanta Metropolitan Bureau of Investigation had determined that Salerno was in Atlanta alone and had stuck close to Margo's building. They were betting that no phones were tapped.

He also said that a check with the phone company revealed that Salerno had called a Chicago pay phone at 1:00 A.M. "There's no way of knowing," Barnes said, "but we think he called Judge Franklin."

Haymeyer advised us to maintain a normal routine for the day, so Margo and I planned to go out for dinner, then go to my apartment so I could do some more sketches before the evening service. I was to have her back at her apartment in time for the bogus phone call at nine o'clock. Haymeyer said he would get more instructions to us during the afternoon.

"I have a new appreciation for hunted animals," Margo said at dinner. "Honestly, Philip, I feel so vulnerable, and I have the strangest feeling for Mr. Salerno."

"*Mr.* Salerno?"

"I suppose that sounds a bit too respectful, doesn't it? I have no respect for him, of course, but have you ever wondered what kind of background a man like that must have had? Was he ever loved? Ever cared about? Ever disciplined? I mean, he's not the troublemaker type, not just an attention seeker. He's the opposite. He's smart and quiet and motivated—by what?"

"Money."

"But is that all? Isn't something missing? Could just money be worth giving up conscience? He has prestige only among a tiny group of people. Does he have a wife, a family?"

"I don't know," I said, as if I didn't care. I realized that I didn't, at least not as much as Margo seemed to. "Why do you care, Margo?"

"I don't know. I really don't. A week ago, a month ago for sure, I wouldn't have cared at all. I might even have been capable of killing a man who wanted to kill me. I know I was capable of killing myself. I almost did. I would have if God hadn't sent you there.

"That must be it, Philip. I was capable of killing because I hated myself. Antonio Salerno must have a terrible self-image. He must hate himself to be capable of hating another person enough to murder him."

"You were brutally honest with me last night, Margo, and I think I learned a lot about myself from it. So, let me be honest. I can't seem to muster any concern over *Mr.* Salerno as you call him. He's sin personified, and he needs to be dealt with."

"How does God deal with sin?"

"He judges it. His wrath comes down upon it. He is righteous and will not tolerate it."

"Wrong."

Margo sounded smug. Here was a day-old Christian telling me I was wrong about the judgment of God. "I'm not wrong, Margo. You are."

"Did God judge you or me, Philip? Weren't you trying to convince me for days that God is a God of love? Does God love Tony Salerno, or does He love only you and me?"

"We're talking about a two-bit free-lance artist and a manic-depressive, possibly suicidal daughter of a socialite as opposed to a professional killer! I'm not saying God can't love Salerno. I'm just saying God hates his sin and Salerno's probably past the point of no return." I knew when I said it that I was wrong. If God loved everyone and offered a free gift to all who would receive it, then that would have to include a mob hit man as well. Margo was going to be one intriguing Christian, taking God at His word right down the line.

"I don't know about you, Philip, but I'm going to try to

show Salerno that God loves him. Not just tell him, but show him."

"How?"

"I'll visit him in prison. I'll do things for him. I'll be so nice to him he won't know what hit him."

"Good grief, Margo. This is morbid. Have you considered the possibility that he may be scared off this time and track you for months?"

"I don't even want to think about it."

"Neither do I."

"Philip, you sound like you're arguing against Christianity."

"I just want to be realistic. After last night, maybe arguing against instead of for would be more appreciated."

"Oh, poor baby," Margo mocked. "Is he hurt because his efforts went unappreciated?"

I said nothing, letting her taunt linger in the air so she could hear how cruel it sounded.

"OK, I probably do owe you an apology for being so confusing last night. I think you got the point, but let's don't talk about being realistic. Had I been realistic, I'd have jumped out the window. There's nothing less realistic than asking God to forgive your sin and Christ to be your Lord."

"Until you've done it," I said. "Then it makes sense."

"Exactly," Margo said. "We agree."

I wasn't so sure.

We continued our discussion at my apartment, and I got no sketching done. "Is there a chance that we're arguing and playing games with semantics because we're both scared to death?" I asked.

"I'm sure that's true," Margo said. "I'm sorry." She sounded beat.

"You're tired," I said.

"Yes, I sure am," she said, staring out the window and talking in a monotone. "Can we go for a ride?"

I said I guessed it would be considered routine for us to take a Sunday afternoon drive. I assumed she wanted to nap, but not in my apartment—and certainly not in hers. Barnes and Warren were waiting there for Salerno to leave her building just for a few minutes, for a paper or something, anything, so they could get in and plant a dummy. We were to stay away.

Margo leaned her head against the car door window and was asleep before we'd gone a mile. She felt secure with me, in a car, and moving. I didn't, I felt followed—and I was.

At first I thought I was being overly sensitive. Sure, the same gray sedan had been behind me for a long time, but that could be coincidence. The guy was probably just going my way. After about ten miles on the freeway, I decided to take a familiar exit so I could determine for sure that it was only my imagination. I didn't want to get into a section of town that would pen me in if I did need to keep some distance between me and whoever was tailing me.

I exited about one hundred yards ahead of the gray car and waited at a light to turn right. Just as the light changed I caught a glimpse of him in my rearview mirror. It was a Plymouth, and he was exiting too. I turned right and kept my eye on the mirror to see if he'd follow. I let my breath out slowly when he went straight through the intersection. My heart pounded. False alarm.

I took another right to head back to the freeway. He had taken two quick rights and was behind me again, closer now. His sun visor was down so I couldn't see him well. He was a block behind and maintained the distance as we both turned right again onto the freeway.

I accelerated but he matched my speed. Margo stirred. "Where are we?" she asked.

"Nowhere special," I said, shakily. "Just driving." She looked at me hard and long. I tried to smile and determined not to look in the rearview mirror while she was watching. She put her head back down and closed her eyes. I shot a glance at the mirror. The gray car was almost in my blind spot to my left rear. What would he do on a busy expressway?

I alternated between the two middle lanes every half mile or so, pretending not to see him. I didn't want to give him the chance of running me off the road. There was no way he'd dare take a shot while driving. Besides endangering himself, he'd have bad odds of a direct hit.

I signaled and moved into the left center lane. For the first time he moved behind me and up on the right. Margo's side of the car. I couldn't let him get even with her. I shot into his lane, sending him into a long screeching slide and rolling Margo nearly into my lap.

"What's happening?" she screamed.

"Stay down! I think it's Salerno!" I put the pedal to the floor and moved into the far right lane ahead of a semi, whose driver blasted me with his air horn. An exit appeared on my right and I began a long swerve to make it while riding the brakes to pull back from about eighty miles an hour. The mirror showed the gray Plymouth passing the semi on the shoulder and exiting a couple of hundred feet behind me.

I hit the accelerator again, only to jump on the brakes, and skid up to the pump at the gas station. "Stay down!" I told Margo as curious heads turned from inside and outside the station. The Plymouth went past the station and came in from a far entrance, pulling up on the other side of the same pump from the opposite direction. The door of the Plymouth flew open and the driver lunged out. I slammed my car in drive and was about to speed off when I saw his face.

It was Haymeyer, and he was furious.

"Follow me back to my hotel!" he said, teeth clenched. He drove away in the Plymouth as I sat with my arms at my sides, forehead resting on the steering wheel, and Margo staring at me, saying nothing.

"Fill'er up, sir?" a young boy said, knocking on my window.

I shook my head slowly and drove out of the station. Just as I pulled onto the street the car coughed and died. I was out of gas.

"Rub it in," I told Margo on the way to Haymeyer's. "Enjoy yourself. Tell me how stupid it was to assume it was Salerno."

"I thought it was him too," she said. "And I don't get any enjoyment from your stupidity—I didn't mean that. I mean, I don't think you're stupid. I think you're wonderful."

"You're tired," I said.

"Yes, but I won't apologize for saying that. You are wonderful."

"You're humoring me. Don't."

"I give up."

"Don't do that either."

"Well, Philip, it's just that you can dish it out but you can't take it. You tell me for weeks that I'm somebody, that I'm worth caring about. God uses you to teach me that, I tell you that you almost got in the way of His message, and you figure I don't appreciate you. You're wrong. I appreciate you. I treasure you. Can't you just let me tell you that without saying I'm patronizing you?"

"OK," I said. "I'm wonderful." We laughed.

"I'm scared," Margo said.

"So am I."

"What took you so long?" Haymeyer asked as he opened his motel room door.

"I figured I'd get gas as long as I was there," I said. Margo stifled a giggle.

"Why were you following us?"

"Didn't you realize we were keeping you under constant watch?" Haymeyer said. "Honestly, Philip, sometimes I think you know what's going on and that you might even be an asset, and then you pull something like this. Had I wanted to follow you without your knowing it, I would have. I stayed in plain sight so you'd know. Didn't you recognize the car? You rode in it the first day I was here."

"That was at night," I said.

Haymeyer shook his head. "Is there somewhere you can go until this thing is over?" he asked.

I shook my head. "Not unless you want me to go to Dayton."

"Maybe we should all go back to Chicago to try to track down Olga, and we could leave Salerno down here alone. You'd like that, wouldn't you?"

Haymeyer was still furious, and I didn't know whether to take him seriously or not. "I'd like what—going to Chicago or leaving Salerno alone?"

Haymeyer turned his palms up and rolled his eyes toward heaven. "What did I do to deserve this?"

Margo was smiling.

"Margo would like to see Salerno left alone," I said. She fired a double take at me.

Her smile was gone. "If you think *that,* you missed my whole point," she said.

"All right, all right," Haymeyer said. "Let's stay cool. Margo's going through a normal reaction of concern for her stalker. You're both jumpy. Philip, I was kidding about your leaving town, especially to go to Chicago. Salerno would be onto us for sure.

"Right now he's holed up in his apartment at Margo's building. He did go out early this afternoon for about a half hour, and the dummy has been planted.

"Now both of you listen very carefully. After church tonight, Philip, take Margo home as usual. Walk her to her door. See her inside and then leave. Do not linger or look back. Go to your car and head straight for my motel. Ask the desk clerk for a message, and a key will be in the envelope I have left for you there. Go to my room and wait. Keep the door locked, but be ready to open it immediately should you hear Barnes's voice.

"Margo, when you get inside your apartment, don't be startled by the dummy in your chair. Turn on a few lights and the TV and leave immediately. Take the east stairs down four floors and go down the hall to the west stairs, which will take you down three more flights to the basement garage. When you get to the garage, Barnes will pull up in a dark green

Ford four-door. When you're sure it's him, get in the back door and lie down on the seat until he tells you to sit up. He'll take you to my motel room and will stay there with you and Philip."

Haymeyer repeated the instructions word for word, then added: "Maybe you two can teach Barnes how to pray and the three of you can pray for Warren and me. We want to catch Salerno *in* the apartment. If it works any other way, we won't have him on anything serious enough to make him talk."

We didn't hear much of the sermon that night. We had our own concerns in mind during the prayer too.

"How are they going to be sure Salerno doesn't see me leave?" Margo asked as we drove to her place.

"Haymeyer figures Salerno will watch us come in from somewhere in the lobby downstairs. He'll sit tight there until he sees me leave. Then he'll head for your apartment. Since you're leaving right after I do, you'll be gone by the time he gets there."

"How do they know he won't take the stairs?"

"They're hoping he'll think it would look too suspicious."

"I don't know what I think about all this figuring and hoping," Margo said.

"They're not amateurs, Margo," I said.

As we walked through the lobby of her building to the elevators, I saw Salerno. He wore denim and low-cut boots. His hair was combed straight back and was darker than his blond mustache. He wore tinted eyeglasses and held an unlit cigarette. We walked within six feet of him. He was slouched in an overstuffed chair and never moved or even looked at us, at least until we had our backs to him.

"That was him," I said on the elevator.

"Who?"

"The guy slouched in the chair. That was Salerno."

"I didn't even see him."

"You're kidding."

Margo didn't answer. I wished I hadn't said anything.

Maybe she had held out a hope that he wouldn't show tonight. At least this way she knew he was in the lobby and not lurking down the hall.

I squeezed Margo's hand and whispered that I would be praying for her. "You know what to do, right?" I asked.

She nodded and unlocked her door. I turned and headed toward the elevator. When I got on, Bob Warren got off, nodded to me ever so slightly, and walked down the hall the opposite way from Margo's apartment. I felt better—until I got to the lobby. Salerno was gone. I hoped he had taken another elevator and not the stairs.

I waited at Haymeyer's hotel room for exactly six minutes before I heard Barnes's voice outside the door. "Philip, open up," he said loudly. Once inside, Margo sat on the bed, her face in her hands. Barnes bolted the door.

"Now what?" I said, relieved to see Margo.

"We wait," Barnes said. "And I'm as anxious as you are. We weren't followed. I'm tempted to go back and help, but it'd be over by the time I got there."

"You think so?" I asked.

"Sure. We had Salerno spotted in the lobby when you two walked in. By the time I picked up Margo and drove outside the garage, he was gone."

"I noticed that too," I said.

Barnes nodded. "It won't be long," he said. "Salerno won't spend much time in the apartment." He flipped on the television. "As soon as he fires two shots, he's out of ammunition. All Bob and Earl have to do is wait until he 'murders' the dummy, then they move in and take him."

"You don't think he smelled the stakeout and took off?"

"Nope. Somehow, I don't think he knows we're around."

"Will all those other charges he's been tried for help convict him?"

"No," Barnes said. "He was acquitted. That means, believe it or not, that Antonio Salerno has a record as clean as yours or mine. Wanmacher thought he had Salerno cold at least a half dozen times but never saw a judge put him away. In fact, Wanmacher had Salerno in court so often, Jim Hanlon figures Tony had a motive to kill him."

"That's how Salerno got involved in the Wanmacher case?"

"Yeah, but I think Hanlon knew he didn't do it and just charged him to irritate him and Wahl. Don't tell Earl I said that, even though I think he agrees."

"Hanlon never thought Salerno killed Wanmacher?"

"I don't think so. Sure, Salerno had threatened Wanmacher, and he had a motive of sorts. But a twenty-two between the eyes is not Salerno's style."

From the ten o'clock news on television we heard, "Shots have been fired at the Kenilworth Arms apartment building on Atlanta's south side. More details as they become available." Margo lay on the bed staring at the wall.

Barnes stood quickly and began pacing. "They said shots, plural. If it was only two, they probably got him. If it was more, they may have killed him. We don't want that."

"Could Salerno have shot Earl or Bob?" I asked.

"I doubt it," Barnes said. "They're not amateurs."

"Neither is Salerno," I said.

Barnes pursed his lips and shook his head.

"Does Salerno always empty both barrels?" I asked.

"Always. The first one does the job. The second is his trademark. It's his way of saying, 'I don't shoot and run. I linger and make sure.'"

I glanced at Margo. She appeared catatonic.

Barnes switched channels with every commercial for the next twenty-five minutes, hoping for more news about the shoot-out. Nothing. It was another hour before Haymeyer and Warren returned. Margo was still, I was watching television, and Barnes was reading. We all stood when we heard the key in the door.

"We had Salerno underrated," Warren grumbled as he sat on the floor.

"You mean *I* had him underrated," Haymeyer said. "I never should have expected him to fall for a dummy."

"Start from the beginning," I said. "Did you get him? I want to hear it all."

Warren answered, "Yes, we got him, thanks to Earl. It was close."

"I *had* to salvage it after I realized he was on to the decoy," Haymeyer said.

"C'mon," Barnes said, impatient. "Let's hear it from the top."

"OK," Earl said. "We had men from the Atlanta Bureau stationed on each floor and in the lobby for backup. Another waited just outside the stairwell door near Margo's apartment. Warren was at the other end of the hall, just around the corner. I used the same elevator to the seventh floor that Salerno had used. I was behind him by about a minute-and-a-half.

"When the elevator opened I could see from there that Salerno was in Margo's place and had left the door open about two inches. I expected him to shoot immediately, but after several seconds I turned off the elevator to keep the door open, kicked off my shoes, and tiptoed down the hall. Through the door I saw Salerno sneak up behind the dummy. The TV was loud, and he probably figured Margo hadn't heard him come in. He waited just behind the dummy, and I think it was then that he realized 'Margo' hadn't moved all the time he was in there.

"As he shook the dummy I realized how foolish I had been to try to catch a pro with an old trick, and I knew if he didn't fire, we'd have nothing solid enough on him to make him talk in exchange for a lighter sentence."

"This is where it gets good," Warren said, eyes gleaming.

"Well, we were lucky it worked," Earl said. "I knelt and pulled Margo's door shut, hoping to spook him—"

"And it worked," Warren said, clapping.

Haymeyer continued, "Salerno whirled and fired, blowing

the door knob over my head. I dashed for the elevator and dove in just as Salerno burst through Margo's door and sprayed his second shot down the hall."

"Who shot Salerno?" I asked.

"No one," they said, almost in unison. "When Salerno fired his second shot, he was out of ammunition."

I turned to Haymeyer. "Did he try to run?"

"No way," Earl said. "When we heard that second shot, we all converged on him. He was through. He just dropped his weapon.

"Philip, remember our three objectives?"

"Yeah."

"I think two have been accomplished. We kept you and Margo safe, and we've got something good on Salerno. Now we have to hope he'll sing for his supper."

"Exactly what have you got on Salerno?" I asked. "Since he didn't shoot the dummy, I mean."

"First, we've got him on breaking and entering," Warren said. "You should have seen him. I swear he got in that room quicker and more smoothly than if he'd have a key."

"That's a felony," Earl said. "And possession of a sawed-off shotgun is illegal in any state."

"But the biggie," Warren said, "was when he fired at Earl. The first time he was just shooting through the door, and it might have been hard to prove that he intended anyone bodily harm."

"But when he fired again as I dove into the elevator," Haymeyer chimed in, "that was attempted murder. We'll let him think about that one for awhile. Then we'll see if he'd like to talk about Virginia Franklin."

With that, Margo broke down. Haymeyer put her arm around her. "You've been tight for a few days. Let it out."

"You don't understand," Margo managed. "None of you do. Don't you see? My mother tried to have me killed. I didn't really believe it until you described him stalking my dummy. He was going to kill me on orders from my own mother!"

EIGHT

When Margo calmed down, Larry arranged for a room for her at the motel. She went to bed and the rest of us went out for a midnight snack. "This was going to be a celebration," Haymeyer said, "but I can sure see Margo's point. Her own mother. Have you met her, Philip?"

"No. I just met Margo a few weeks ago."

"You want to go to Chicago with us? Margo will have to come anyway."

"She won't go without me," I said.

"We're hoping we can talk Atlanta into delaying arraignment on Salerno until after he can be extradited to Chicago to face charges of conspiracy to commit murder. It might be difficult because attempted murder is really the more serious offense. If we can implicate a judge, we've got two people involved in a very serious crime, though, and the conspiracy happened before the attempted murder."

"What happens in Chicago?"

"Well, we're going to make things very uncomfortable for Mrs. Franklin."

"How?"

"Hanlon hasn't decided yet. If Salerno talks, it will be easy. If he doesn't, Jim may try to get Mrs. Franklin to think Salerno's talked anyway. She's pretty cool though, and she knows the law. She was a great lawyer and judge in her prime."

"Really?"

"Absolutely. She was for sure the most respected trial judge in Illinois."

"Was?"

"Until her marriage went on the rocks and she started bad-mouthing her own daughter in public."

"You're kidding. I don't think Margo is even aware of that!"

"Oh, it was sickening. I guess she was ashamed of her because of her weight. You can't tell it now, Philip, but Margo was somewhat overweight when she was younger. Hanlon used to grouse about it after a social function. He'd come back to the office complaining that Mrs. Franklin was poking fun at her own daughter again."

"What would she say about her?"

"Oh, I don't now. I guess she said she would have brought her daughter to the function if she could find a tent to fit her—stuff like that."

"That's disgusting."

"Yeah, and Philip, being overweight or an embarrassment to a mother is hardly grounds for murder. I believe every word Margo says. The old lady is as guilty as she can be, and I want to help the boss prove it."

"So do I."

"You might be able to help," Haymeyer said. "I never told you what my phone call from Chicago was about the other night, did I?"

"No, but I figured it must have been important, since you didn't want to return it from your room."

"It was about Olga. The Chicago boys traced her through IRS to her son at Northwestern University in Evanston. According to him she's financing his education with money she won from the Illinois State Lottery and is living on Lake Shore Drive under a phony name so her friends won't come asking for money. You don't know Chicago, but Lake Shore Drive is ultra."

"Boy, that was some piece of luck for Olga."

"Yeah, too much luck. She never reported any winnings on her income tax returns, and according to state records she never won a dime."

"Then where's she getting the money to live on Lake Shore and put a son through college?"

"You tell me."

Barnes and Warren left for Chicago the next day. Haymeyer stayed with Margo and took several written depositions, "just so we'll have everything straight when we get to Chicago and have to go through all this again."

Haymeyer told me he was sure Margo was out of danger but advised me to keep her at the motel until I could drive her to Chicago. He left on Tuesday with instructions that we should be in Chicago within a week. "Better have her quit her job and get out of her lease," he advised. "I doubt she'll be back here for a long time."

The day Haymeyer left I got a check for $4,000 for my textbook sketches. It was the most money I had ever received at one shot, but I could hardly get excited.

Margo spent most of her time at the motel unless she was out eating with me or watching me sketch. She wanted to rest before making the trip, and that was fine with me. What wasn't fine was her insistence on visiting Tony Salerno at the county jail. I refused to even hear of it. I was to know where she was every second, but on Friday, when I couldn't find her at the motel or the restaurant or anywhere, I felt down deep that she had gone to see Salerno.

When I got to the House of Corrections I toured the parking lot for about twenty minutes before spotting her car. I raced inside and asked if Margo Franklin had been admitted to visit a prisoner.

"Yes, sir, about a half hour ago. She's still there."

"I want to see the same man," I said. "I'm a friend of Margo's." I was searched, authorized, stamped, badged, and read a list of regulations. Four heavy doors later I saw Margo, sitting, waiting.

"I'm sorry, Philip, I had to come."

"Have you seen him yet?"

"No, he's talking with his lawyer."

"Wahl is here, huh? I'll bet they're trying to get him out on bond, or at least push for his extradition to Chicago. That's home to these guys, and I'll bet they think they've got a better chance beating the conspiracy charge. There's no way they'll beat the attempted murder charge here. The longer they can put that off, the better they'll like it."

Margo seemed relieved that I was off the subject of her being at the jail, but I came back to it. "What do you think you're going to accomplish?" I asked.

"I've told you before. I feel for Salerno. I want to tell him that he is loved, even that I love him."

"Good grief, Margo, this isn't a game. All he has to do is tell Wahl that you visited, and your mother will be the next to know. Haymeyer doesn't want your mother to know that you were involved in helping nail Salerno."

"You don't think she knows already?"

"I would have thought so, but Haymeyer thinks she'll assume that he trailed Salerno here at Hanlon's request and that Salerno was careless."

"Oh, Philip, if she's following developments at all she knows my apartment got shot up. How could I have not known what was going on?"

"She still won't know that you know she's involved."

"How will my visiting Salerno prove that I know she's involved?"

"I don't know," I admitted. "OK, I still think it's a bad idea for you to talk to Salerno, but if you're determined to go through with it, at least keep quiet about your mother."

Margo seemed to relax, realizing that I was not going to try to keep her from seeing Salerno. It would have done no good. She had a mind of her own and knew what she wanted. Who was I to tell her what to do? "At least let me be with you when you talk to him," I said.

We saw Salerno through safety glass and talked to him through telephones. Wahl was with him, a bit too pleased to see us. He talked first. "I suppose you're wondering about what happened in your apartment the other night, young lady." Margo stared at him. "Simply a case of mistaken identity. Had nothing to do with you. My client doesn't even know you. You don't know him, do you?"

Margo and I looked at each other. Wahl beamed. Salerno never took his eyes from Margo's. How could Wahl expect us to be so naive? How did he think a dummy had been planted without Margo having known she was being stalked?

"Hope that clears it up for you kids," Wahl concluded. It was ludicrous.

"I want to talk to him," Margo said, pointing at Salerno. Wahl handed him the phone. "I want you to know that God loves you and that I love you, Mr. Salerno. No matter what you go through the next several weeks, I want you to always know that someone loves you." Salerno never moved. He just stared. He said nothing. The scene reminded me of when I had first met Margo. For some reason I had loved the unlovable. Now she was doing the same, only to an infinitely greater degree.

Wahl was still smiling and Salerno staring as we left. Margo was boiling. "I wanted so badly to demand to know if my mother had told him to do it," she said, her eyes afire. "And that Wahl! There's one I haven't been given any love for yet. Pray for me."

"Pray for *me*," I said. "I still haven't seen anything in Salerno but a creep."

When we got back to my apartment I called Haymeyer in Chicago. "You shouldn't have let that happen," he said when I told him of our visit to Salerno. "I was counting on you. Can you get Margo to Chicago, or should I send someone for her?" He was being sarcastic, and it smarted.

"We're leaving tomorrow," I said.

"You can bet old lady Franklin knows all about your visit already. No doubt Wahl keeps in close contact."

Haymeyer told us to come directly to United States Attorney Hanlon's office when we arrived in Chicago. "If for some crazy reason Wahl and Mrs. Franklin think Margo really isn't aware of the plot, let's keep them thinking it. We'll have Margo keep a low profile here for a while."

Margo and I took turns driving my car and got to Chicago late Saturday night. "It sounds crazy," she said sleepily, "but I have this desire to see Mother, being so close and all."

"You mean you really would like to confront her?"

"No, just see her. I remember her as she was, not as she is. I don't know the woman she has become. Even during my teen years when I felt rejected by her, there was a lot of Mommy left in her, in spite of herself. After Richard was murdered, she became an animal, never the same. I can't dwell on it, Philip. I may never be able to. To think that she would have me killed! Do you realize that it was only the chance timing of our letter to Hanlon that saved my life?"

"I guess you're right," I said.

"That was God, Philip."

"Right again."

It was nearly midnight, and we were tired, but Margo insisted on showing me a reminder of her childhood. We drove north on Lake Shore Drive toward Evanston.

"So this is where Olga lives, huh?" I said. "In one of these big, dark buildings. I hope she's enjoying it. They don't look like they're worth that much money."

"It's not the building or the furnishings," Margo said. "It's the location. Lake Shore Drive is the place to be if you want to flaunt it."

Farther north, Evanston was beautiful. "It always is at night," Margo said. There was a quaintness about it, street lights on ancient poles, eight-bedroom mansions guarding acre lots.

"This looks more like the place to flaunt it," I said. Margo didn't respond.

A few miles north Lake Shore Drive reached Sheridan Road which was darker and more winding. "It's just around the next curve," she said.

"What is?" I said, just as it broke into view. The Baha'i temple gleamed majestically against the blackness of the night sky. It was like a three-dimensional picture card I'd looked at through a special lens box as a child—breathtaking.

"What faith is it, Margo?"

"I never checked into it much," she said. "It was just here. It was God to me. People came to look, and I guess they even held services, but I never went. It was so beautiful that I was afraid of it. I guess it was like the Wizard of Oz to Dorothy. So powerful, so awesome that it was frightening. I longed to know the God of this place, but I resented the fear it instilled in me when I walked around it at night.

"When no one else was near, it seemed as if I were being watched as I walked. Can we walk?"

"It's late, Margo. Are you sure you want to?"

She was sure. I parked and we walked around the temple. It was after one o'clock in the morning, but we were not alone. There were a few couples and a family or two, just walking, looking. No one spoke. It was eerie. I felt for Margo and her childhood fears. Nothing made the temple look real. Not from any angle. It could have vanished with my next blink. But it didn't. It loomed bright and yet shadowy, its dome lighting the sky, its pillars posing questions for young debutantes who gazed at it while walking alone at night. Their families were worshipers of things, goods, money, prestige, power, position. The young girls knew already that those were symbols of the shallowness of life.

If there was something in the temple, they wanted it. If there was nothing, they would resign themselves to the battle for position and forget their childish wonderment at the glistening monolith.

"How does it look in the daytime?" I asked.

"Like it's waiting for the night."

Margo drove on the way back to Chicago. She took a left off the main drag. "Where you headed?"

"Home," she said.

"Margo."

"Don't worry, Philip. I just want to see the place, and I want you to see it. It's only a few blocks from here." She took me through a heavily wooded area and into a section where the huge homes weren't so far apart. "That's it, there, through the trees."

"Wow. Your mother still lives there alone?"

"Yeah, isn't that weird? I imagine she entertains, and no doubt she has live-in help. But otherwise, she's alone."

"How many bedrooms?"

"Just seven."

"*Just* seven? Margo, that's the Winnetka in you. There's a light on."

"Yes, in my old bedroom!"

"Who would be in there at this time of night?"

"Who else?" Margo said. "Is it too much to hope that Mother is sitting on my bed, crying over how near she came to having me killed and thankful now that Salerno failed?"

It was too much to ask, and I barely heard her last few words as she swallowed her sobs. I was tired; we both were. She pulled off the road and fell into my arms. We held each other and cried for several minutes. I felt so sorry for her that I would have given anything for it all to have been a nightmare. "We've got to get going, Margo."

I got out and went around to the driver's side while Margo slid over. Elbows on knees, she held her face in her hands and cried softly all the way back to Chicago. I rented us each a room at a downtown Holiday Inn and handed over her key without a word.

"How's she holding up?" Haymeyer asked in the morning after pulling me aside at the United States attorney's office.

"I'm not sure," I said. "She took me to Winnetka last night, and it was hard on her."

"She didn't want to drop in on the old lady, did she?"

"No, but we went by there well after midnight and a light was on in Margo's old room."

"Wow."

Haymeyer introduced us to James A. Hanlon, the United States attorney for Northern Illinois, and it took me a while to get used to his plush office. He was a stocky six-footer with a reputation for incorruptibility.

"Earl has told me a lot about you, Philip Spence," Hanlon said, carefully enunciating both names. "You can't do anything officially, of course, but the rest of this investigation will be quite tame compared to the Atlanta activity. I see no reason why you can't tag along, *if you agree to be under the supervision and direction of this office whenever you are with one of my agents.*" He had a way of talking in italics.

"I understand," I said, tingling. "Fine." I could hardly wait to get started. "Where will Margo be during the investigation?"

"Sometimes with you, sometimes not," Hanlon said. "Your rooms at the Inn are fine with us. Just stay accessible. She is technically in our custody, and this case could go to court anytime."

"Have charges been filed?"

"No, we're waiting until we've got it all but locked up."

"What will that take?"

"Something good from Salerno, or from this Yakovich woman, or from the judge herself."

"Which looks most promising?"

"None. Salerno and his jackass lawyer are claiming he was pulling a petty theft—with a sawed-off yet—and was unaware of any connection between the occupant of the apartment and the judge who had recently thrown his case out of court. The judge has not been contacted by this office, though I imagine she's expecting us. She doesn't know Margo's in town, though, and we want to keep it that way."

"And Olga?"

"She would be our best chance because she's not a professional from either side of the law, but we still haven't found her. Her son might be the key. He's sworn to secrecy about her address, and you know, I think he believes her story about the lottery. If we surprise him by telling him what's at stake, he may just be shocked into putting us onto his mother."

"It might scare him into tipping her off, though," I said.

"It'll depend on how we do it, Philip. You wanna go along?"

"Sure."

Jon Yakovich was earnest, a bit irritated, and very concerned. "I already told my story," he objected.

"I know," said Haymeyer, "but I was out of town and didn't get to hear it. Hit us with it again."

Jon said his mother had won money in the state lottery and was financing his education with it, saving some, and living in anonymity on Lake Shore Drive with the rest.

"Can't you tell us where, Jon? There are thousands of people on the Drive. We'll go door to door if we have to, but it could take months."

"Why should I? She wants to remain hidden. If her friends find out where she is, they'll beg for money. The worst part is, she'd probably give it to them. She's a generous person."

"Then why doesn't she let them know?"

"I don't know. It surprises me too," Jon said. "She once said that if she ever came into a lot of money, she'd give most of it away. Maybe she's changed her mind because she feels she needs it. Once she told me she felt she deserved it after all she'd been through—coming from the old country, Dad dying twenty years ago."

"Could there be another reason she doesn't want her friends to know, Jon?"

"What are you suggesting?"

"That she didn't get the money from the lottery, and that if her friends found out about it, they might also find out where she got it."

"What are you saying?"

"I'm saying that most people who win the lottery are happy to share the news and that a person like your mother would be happy to even share some of her winnings."

"Maybe that's true, but what does it prove? Where else could she have gotten the money?"

"Didn't she work for rich people on the north shore?"

"Yes, but she hated them. She always resented their money and how little it seemed to mean to them. They wouldn't have given her anything. When she first got a job up there in Winnetka she thought it would be the chance of a lifetime. But they were so tight they paid her less than people in Chicago. Can you imagine?"

"Did that upset her?"

"Yes, it did. She was extremely angry in her own way. She brooded."

"Would it have made her mad enough to steal some money?"

Jon stared at Haymeyer. "No," he said finally.

"You say that with conviction."

"Well, I know because she used to look for money. She hoped they'd leave cash around that she could lift unnoticed."

"Then she wouldn't be above taking money?"

"No, so what? She had a hard life. She always wanted me to have an education. Her daughters both died at birth. She is a tired, bitter, hard-working old woman. The lottery was a gift from God."

"Oh, come on, Jon. You don't believe she won the lottery, do you?"

"Why don't I?"

"Did you ever know her to buy a lottery ticket?"

Jon didn't answer. "What do you want her for?" he asked. "Stealing lottery tickets?"

"It's not funny, Jon. Your mother could be in very big trouble."

"What kind of trouble?"

"Big and serious. If she is involved in something bad, we have reason to believe she could help us and do herself some good."

"Tell me what it is and I'll tell you where to find her."

"Let's do it the other way around, Jon. You tell us where, and we'll tell you what."

"No deal."

"It's up to you. We'll find her on our own, but the longer we wait, the harder it will be for her to get a break."

"At least she'll know I didn't send you to her."

"And we'll tell her you could have made things a lot easier for her."

"She'll understand," Jon said.

"She'll have a long time to think about it," Haymeyer said. He left his business card.

"We'll have a message from Jon waiting for us when we get back to the office," Haymeyer predicted in the car. He was right.

"You make sure Mother knows why I sent you to her, for her own good, but don't tell me what it's about. She wouldn't want me to know. If she wants to tell me, she can." He gave us an address.

No one answered our knock. We waited at the end of the hall for six hours before a short woman with black-dyed hair and a plain beige coat trudged from the elevator to her apartment door carrying a twine-handled shopping bag in each hand. She set them down to fish for her keys, and Haymeyer moved in.

He flashed his badge and identified himself as a special agent for the United States attorney's office. "Olga Yakovich?"

"No," she said huskily. "Don't know no Yakovich."

"Do you know Jon Yakovich?" Haymeyer needled.

"What's the matter with my Jon?" she demanded. "Come in. Talk to me. What is problem with Jon?"

"No problem, Olga," Haymeyer said. "We just wanted to be sure it was you."

Olga put her groceries away, looking totally out of place in the beautifully furnished apartment. Her clothes were plain and off the rack. She wore no jewelry. She sat heavily on the sofa.

"Jon send you to me?" she asked with a whine.

"For your own good, Mrs. Yakovich. He didn't want you in trouble. He doesn't know why we want to see you."

"Olga don't know either," she said, glaring.

"Yes, you do."

"No."

"We want to know where a housekeeper gets the money to live here and send her son to Northwestern University."

"Lottery. I win three-hundred thousand dollars. Get some every month. You check bank account."

"We have, Olga. We have also checked your income tax reports. You haven't paid taxes on your winnings."

"I am ignorant old woman. I know nothing of taxes."

"You are not ignorant, but letting your income show in your bank account without paying income tax was stupid."

"So what's wrong?"

"You didn't win the lottery, and stop insisting you did. We have access to those records."

"I didn't have name listed because I wanted friends not to know."

"Get off the case, Olga. We have access to the actual records. You did not win, and no money has come to you from the state of Illinois. Where are you getting your money?"

"Why should I tell you?"

"If you tell us and help us get who we're really after, we might be able to help you get a better deal from the law."

"And if I don't tell you?"

"We'll find out soon enough, and there will be no mercy for you."

"I think about it."

"Don't think too long, Olga. We're working on this around the clock. You help us, and we'll help you."

"Why didn't Judge Franklin send Salerno after Olga?" I asked Haymeyer on the way back to the office.

"She's probably got a system that would bring information to light if she is harmed. It's not hard to do. It could be through her bank, a lawyer, or even her son. If she is killed, a document is publicized, probably implicating Mrs. Franklin."

"How much is she hitting Mrs. Franklin for?"

"About three thousand a month."

I whistled through my teeth. "What's next?"

"We'll have to put a little pressure on Olga, I think," Haymeyer said. "She's tough and smarter than she appears. She knows we have little without her, and she's not likely to come to us. We're going to have to scare her, trick her, or convince her."

"I like option number three."

"That's the idealist in you, Philip. This is where our job gets tedious, but there are no shortcuts. The tough ones never get handed to us on a platter. We've got to go after them."

"I think I'll stick to art."

Hanlon wanted to know how Haymeyer planned to pressure Olga.

"What do you suggest?" Haymeyer replied.

"It sounds to me like Jon could help, if he knew the whole story, straight, with no games, no guessing. You come right out and tell him, blow his mind. Let him see it right there on the table so he doesn't have to guess at the consequences."

Haymeyer studied his boss. I nodded and Hanlon caught it from the corner of his eye. "You agree, Philip?"

"I'm closer to his age," I said. "I think I'd buckle and help put pressure on my mother in the same situation."

"Why don't you talk to Jon alone, Philip?" Hanlon asked.

Haymeyer straightened up. I looked at him, eyebrows raised. "I'm not against it," Earl said. "It just took me by surprise."

Hanlon smiled. "It's up to you, Earl, of course. This is your investigation."

"You're the boss, Jim," Haymeyer said. "If you think this will work, I'm for it."

"The important thing is whether you think it will work," Hanlon said.

"I'm just wishing I'd thought of it, that's all," Haymeyer said.

We all laughed.

That night I took Margo out for dinner and told her all about my day. "It was really exciting. I felt like a detective."

"Did you ask Olga any questions?"

"Not one. They didn't let me get involved at all. But tomorrow I have an appointment with Jon Yakovich again. It should be interesting. I'll keep you posted."

"Could I go too?"

"Hm. I doubt it. I'll check with Haymeyer. What would be the advantage? Did you know Jon?"

"No," Margo said.

"What would you think about dropping in on Olga eventually?"

"I'd have to think about that one. It would sure have impact, wouldn't it?"

"The only problem is that at this point, Olga thinks Haymeyer is fishing. She doesn't realize that he already knows the answers and is simply looking for her to confirm them. She thinks he is simply aware that she is getting her money from somewhere other than the lottery. Your showing up would tell her immediately that she has been found out."

"But without actually saying so to her, Philip. It might be a great move. I think I could do it."

"I'll talk to Haymeyer and Hanlon."

"Well, what do *you* think?"

"I think it might be valuable if it becomes necessary, Margo."

"What is the alternative?"

"Just my seeing Jon for now."

"I'd like to be involved," Margo said.

"Why?"

"Not for revenge, if that's what you think. I just want this mess over with."

"I believe *that*. How are you doing?"

Margo shifted in her chair. "I'm OK, I guess. I'm praying a lot. Reading my Bible. Losing weight."

"I noticed."

"You did not."

"No, really, I did."

"You didn't say anything."

"Well, it isn't like you had much to lose."

"I need to hear it."

"OK, you look like you've lost weight."

Margo laughed. "I think about you all day," she said.

"That's the kind of stuff *I* need to hear."

"I pray for you too. Are you praying for me?"

"Yes, I think of you often and pray that God will comfort you and give you something out of this. I don't see what good can come of it, but I am willing to trust Him for it."

"Maybe He'll give me you out of this," she said carefully.

"That was rather bold."

"Do I care?"

"Obviously not. But you've already got me, Margo, and you know it."

NINE

"Do not, I repeat, do *not* tell Margo where Olga lives," United States Attorney Hanlon said the next morning.

"I didn't," I said.

"See that you don't," Haymeyer horned in.

"I said I won't already!" I said, rolling my eyes.

"Good grief, Earl, is this kid gonna screw us up on this?" Hanlon said. "Because if he is, maybe we'd be better off—"

"He won't, Jim. He didn't really tell her anything important." Haymeyer turned to me. "But don't tell her much of anything from here on out, OK?"

I nodded.

"If she goes to see Olga, it could cost us the whole case. Can you see Jon Yakovich without telling Margo about it?"

"Sure. I already told her I was going to see him, but I won't—" Hanlon and Haymeyer swore in unison.

"He's not catching on, Earl," Hanlon said. "Tell him he simply can't say anything to anyone. This is a highly confidential federal investigation of very serious charges."

Hanlon was telling Haymeyer what to tell me as if he didn't want anything to do with me.

"Do we have to tell you every little tidbit that's confidential, Philip?" Haymeyer asked.

"No."

"I'd be glad to, but I thought you'd know."

"Well, Earl, you told Margo lots of stuff in Atlanta. I figured it was OK to tell her because she's involved."

"You have no idea how much I didn't tell her. Or you either, for that matter."

"Me? What don't I know about this?"

Hanlon and Haymeyer glanced at each other. Haymeyer raised his eyebrows. Hanlon nodded. "This is confidential now," Haymeyer said, as if I didn't know. "It seems that Wahl and Salerno are pushing for extradition to Chicago."

"That's not really a surprise, is it?" I asked. "I mean they've got a better chance up here than down there, don't they?"

"Yes, but that's not the reason they want to come here. They know they'll be coming here anyway. The key is, they want to come immediately."

"So?"

"So, why would they want to come immediately? It seems they'd want to stretch this thing out as long as possible, right?"

"I guess," I said.

"The problem," Haymeyer explained, "is that Salerno's life was threatened last night."

"In the Atlanta jail?"

"Yup. There's no faster grapevine than behind bars. Someone found out why he was there and threatened to do him in tonight after dark."

"For shooting at a cop?" I asked. "Wouldn't they be proud of him?"

"Not for that," Haymeyer said patiently. "For attempting to kill a woman."

"You mean there's some sort of code?"

"Absolutely. No women or children."

Hanlon tipped his chair back. "We can't have him moved up here in one day, but we can't risk someone nailing him either. We're asking Atlanta to put him in solitary confinement until the day after tomorrow. By the time he gets here, he'll already have a roommate."

"A roommate?"

"A cellmate. One of our guys. Larry Shipman is a sort of free-lance police reporter for a couple of the papers and radio stations here, and he does some undercover work for us now and then too. Very little of what he gets for us can be used in court, because he gets it any way he can, but it sure helps us know where we stand."

"I don't follow."

"For instance," Haymeyer said, "he might just come right out and ask Salerno for a lot of information. Even if he got it on tape, Salerno could say he had just been bragging. We'll send Shipman in anyway and see if he can get anything out of Salerno."

Hanlon and Haymeyer had agreed that I should visit Jon Yakovich alone. I found him in his room on the third floor of the dorm and asked if he wanted to take a walk with me. "Not if you're going to tell me about Mama," he said.

"I just want to ask you some questions."

"We can do that here."

I said OK, but before I could sit, he grabbed his jacket and I followed him out. We walked diagonally across the campus. It was dark, yet majestic, and clouds were moving quickly overhead.

"Storm's coming," Jon said finally, his feathery blond hair flying.

"Your mother is in deep trouble," I said. "And if she doesn't tell the U.S. attorney's office what she knows, they may find out anyway and she could go to jail for blackmail."

Jon stopped short and whirled around. "Blackmail?" he repeated, incredulous. He smiled faintly. Either it was impossible to believe, or he was proud of his mother for pulling it off. "You don't mean blackmail," he said.

"That's exactly what I mean," I said, and I told him the whole story quickly. Jon sat on a bench and tucked both feet under him. "It sounds to me like this Judge Franklin is in bigger trouble than Mama," he said.

"For sure. That's why if your mother helps us nail Mrs. Franklin, she could do herself a lot of good."

"She's pretty well off now, wouldn't you say?"

I shook my head. "No, I sure wouldn't."

"And you want me to talk to her, convince her to tell what she knows?"

I nodded.

"How much good will she do herself?" he asked.

"No promises," I said.

"None?"

"Only that if she doesn't talk, she'll suffer eventually."

"That means I will too," Jon said as thunder rolled in the distance. "She's been a good mother. Maybe I can help her."

Jon had promised he'd talk to his mother that evening, but as Hanlon, Haymeyer, the newly introduced Shipman, and I waited for his call, prospects appeared dim. Shipman was more articulate than he appeared. He was scruffy, knowledgeable about police matters, and very much in love with newspaper work. "I'm taking Larry down to have him booked at the county jail," Hanlon said. "You can reach me by radio if I'm not back when Yakovich calls."

By the time Hanlon returned, Larry Shipman was alone in a cell built for two, waiting for Salerno.

"Yakovich called just after you left, Jim," Haymeyer said. "He told his old lady he knew everything and that she should cooperate. She told him he was no son of hers if he believed such things and ordered him out of her apartment. He's pretty shook up."

"What do you think?" Hanlon asked.

"I think she'll be calling us," Haymeyer said.

Margo was angry that I had been advised not to tell her what had gone on. "I'm going crazy here," she said. "I pray, I read my Bible, I think about you. Now I can't know what's going on?"

"I'm sorry," I said.

"I know it's not your fault, Philip. But can't you tell me something if I promise not to do anything or tell anyone else?"

"Who would you tell?"

"Good question. Can't you tell me then?"

"No."

"Oh, Philip! I'm not kidding, this is driving me nuts."

I called Haymeyer at home. "Sorry to bother you," I said, "but can't we do something for Margo's sake? It's too much for her to be in the dark about everything."

"What does she want to do, talk to her mother?" Haymeyer suggested sarcastically.

"Hey," I said, "how about if she talked to her father?" I tried to say it quietly, but Margo spun around, nodding so vigorously that her hair fell beside her face.

Haymeyer was silent for several seconds. I waited. "Let me check with Hanlon on this," he said finally.

Margo was ecstatic. "Oh, thank you, Philip! I haven't talked with Daddy since Atlanta—"

"Haymeyer's just checking, Margo. You know the odds are against it."

"I know they'll let me see him," she said, ignoring me. "I just know it." She turned on the television.

"I think I'll wait in my room," I said. "It won't look good, our being in the same room."

"To whom?" Margo asked mischievously.

"To your father," I said. She threw a cushion at me as I left.

I was exhausted and fell asleep within minutes after stretching out on my bed. I slept fitfully, images playing in my mind. Margo, Jim Barnes, Bob Warren, Earl Haymeyer, James Hanlon, Larry Shipman, Jon Yakovich, Olga, Frederick Wahl, Tony Salerno, my parents. *My parents!* I rolled over and sat up quickly.

What if they had tried calling Atlanta? I flipped the light switch and squinted against the blinding whiteness, groping for the phone.

"I didn't mean to wake you."

I jumped. Someone was in the room! I shielded my eyes and peeked between my fingers. It was Wahl. "I followed you from Hanlon's office," he said, sitting and crossing his legs. He was immaculately dressed, as he had been in Atlanta. My heart cracked so loudly against my chest I could hardly breathe.

"Then you know where Margo is," I said.

"I have no beef with Margo. We made our point to her mother when Salerno got into her apartment in Atlanta."

"You made your point?"

"Yes, I think Mrs. Franklin is convinced that we are capable."

I was confused. "But Salerno blew it in Atlanta."

"For himself, maybe," Wahl said, smiling. "But he wasn't there to hurt the girl anyway. Salerno wouldn't take a job like that. Judge Franklin wanted some proof of our capabilities, that's all. We had to locate her daughter, and then demonstrate that we could kill her, but without hurting her. We did that."

"Salerno wouldn't have killed Margo, even if she *had* been there?"

"No way."

"Why are you telling me this?"

"Proving capabilities again. I could have killed you while you slept."

"You?"

"I *could* have. You understand, I don't do that sort of work myself. I simply see that it gets done."

"I'm not afraid of Salerno, as long as he's in jail."

"Come now, Mr. Spence. You think Tony Salerno is the only man I represent?"

I shrugged. Was I still dreaming? The phone was ringing.

"Don't answer it," Wahl said.

"They'll come for me," I said, feeling like an actor in a B movie.

"I'll be gone by then," Wahl said. He talked fast while the phone rang and rang.

"Our point is this. Mrs. Franklin does not want to be responsible for any more deaths."

"Any *more?*"

"Oh, come on. You know she killed Wanmacher. The point is she doesn't intend to be convicted of that. Without Margo or Olga, they've got nothing on her. That means she has to keep both of them quiet, and, like I said, she doesn't want any more deaths. The money is keeping Olga quiet." He paused meaningfully.

"And what's she gonna do about Margo?"

"We think we've solved that little problem. One of my associates is with her right now. He's telling her that you've been murdered in your room and that she should keep her mouth shut if she doesn't want the same to happen to her father."

"You're going to kill me?"

"Certainly not. I already told you no. I don't do that work. But when I leave, don't be too sure that you're alone."

With that Wahl left, slamming the door.

I froze. Still half prone on the bed, I tried to move without making noise. If I could just bolt through the door before anyone came out of the bathroom or closet. But what if he was under the bed? Or waiting outside the door? And where would I go if I did get out?

I leaned over as far as I could without putting my hand on the floor. The blood rushed to my head as I looked under the bed. I heard a noise. Was it in the closet? The bathroom? Outside? I put one foot on the floor. My chest heaved as I fought to breathe without gasping. Should I turn off the light and take my chances? No, he might have a flashlight and then he could see me without my seeing him. I stood on one foot and edged toward the closet. Maybe I could duck into the closet and he would think I had left. But what if *he* was in the closet?

Should I wait until Haymeyer arrived? But what if it hadn't been Haymeyer on the phone? What if it had been Margo? Would she come up? I couldn't let her. I toyed with just waiting until he made his move, but it seemed hopeless and endless. I prayed silently. *Lord, if it's going to happen, let it happen quickly. Take care of Margo.* Bible verses rang in my head, but they made no sense. They weren't verses of comfort, but rather old standards like Genesis 1:1 and John 3:16.

"Should not perish . . ." hit me as ironic, and I pulled open the closet door. No one. Now I knew he was in the bathroom. Could I do what Haymeyer had done to Salerno? I leaned around the corner. The bathroom door was ajar about three inches. Could I reach it without being seen? Didn't the gunman hear Wahl leave? Why hadn't he come out blasting?

I took three quick steps toward the bathroom door, and though my arm was nearly paralyzed with fear, I grabbed the knob and yanked the door shut. I turned to dive away from the door but slipped on the rug and fell as I heard a banging from the bathroom.

I rolled over and hid my head with my arms, finally realizing that the noise was the soap on a string I had hung on the hook behind the bathroom door. It tapped slower and more softly and then stopped. There was no other noise. I ran to the front door and fastened the chain lock. I went back to the bathroom and listened. Nothing. I opened the door and reached in to turn on the light, causing the soap to bang again and my heart to resound, but no one was there. I collapsed on the tile floor, my back against the bathroom door.

I gasped and every muscle ached. I felt as if I couldn't move, but a loud knock at the front door made me scramble to my feet. I shut and locked the bathroom door, turned off the light, and lay in the bathtub, pulling the shower curtain shut.

The porcelain was cold against my face and hands. I could hear my heart. I prayed that the soap string would quit tapping. Someone was kicking the front door. The lock broke and the chain snapped. I quit breathing.

"Philip!" The voice sounded familiar. I couldn't respond. The soap still swung on the bathroom door. I reached up to pull back the shower curtain as Haymeyer kicked open the door and stood crouching in the darkness, both hands on his gun.

"I'm OK," I managed, as he turned on the light.

He swore. "Someone visited Margo," he said. "She thought you'd been murdered."

"So did I," I said. He helped me out of the tub. I could hardly walk. I flopped onto the bed and Earl called Margo.

"He's OK, Margo. I'll bring him down in a while."

Haymeyer told me he had come to talk Margo out of seeing her father, arriving just after Wahl's man had delivered his threat. Margo had tried to call me, and when she got no answer she ran out of her room and into Haymeyer's arms. She was hysterical. He told her to stay in her room with the door locked, and he bounded up two flights of stairs and down the hall to my room. "I thought you'd had it," he said.

A half hour later Margo and I sat unashamedly with our arms around each other. I stared into her eyes and she cried softly. "They got the desired response," I said.

"What do you mean?" Earl asked.

"I'm through," I said. "I'm willing to leave it alone, take Margo away, and forget it."

"Give it twenty-four hours," Haymeyer said.

"Give it nothing. It's not worth it. Who needs it?"

"You're afraid," Earl said.

"For Margo, yes. Hey, for me too. Sure I'm afraid. I'm scared to death."

"I could kick myself for not being as careful here as we were in Atlanta," Haymeyer said. "But it won't happen again. From now on it's round-the-clock protection for both of you."

I was so wiped out I didn't even bother to argue. We'd get some rest while Haymeyer's men stood guard, and then we'd be long gone.

After Margo and I were moved to adjoining rooms at the Jackson Hotel near the Loop, Jim Barnes, Bob Warren, and another pair of special agents traded off standing guard over us. For the next few days we rested, played word games with our bodyguards, and watched television. We also spent time praying and studying together.

"You're in this as deep as any of us now, Philip," Haymeyer

told me one night. "You've been threatened by the real mouthpiece for the organization in this town. If and when the time comes, I hope you'll testify against him before the grand jury."

"Forget it," I said.

"You're kidding."

"No, I'm not. I already told you, it's not worth it. I'm not going to get shot up or see Margo hurt just to help you bag these creeps."

"Is that what your Bible tells you?" Haymeyer said, looking at me with disgust.

Margo turned to me as if she expected an answer. I shrugged and turned away.

"I'm tempted to withdraw your protection, Philip," Haymeyer said.

"You're not serious."

"I sure am. Why should I protect you? Who are you to me?"

"It's your job to protect a citizen who has been threatened."

"But you haven't been threatened, have you? You're not willing to say you've been threatened, so as far as I am concerned, you haven't been threatened. How long are we supposed to protect you? Forever? We haven't got the men or the money. Someday, unless you help put these guys away, they're going to get you and Margo and anyone else who gets in their way."

I pretended not to hear him, but every word echoed in my brain. I had badgered Margo to come to Chicago at any cost to do what was right. Now, here I was backing out of the most important responsibility I had ever faced. My parents would never believe this. *My parents!*

"How much can I tell my parents?" I asked Haymeyer. "I'd better call them. They've probably been trying to reach me in Atlanta for days."

"Don't tell them anything," Haymeyer said. "Just let them know where you are and that you're here on business."

"Does this mean you're looking for a job?" my mother

wanted to know. "You should check with Mr. Ferguson here in Dayton, Philip."

"I know, Mother. Maybe I will, and I promise I'll come by there before heading south again."

"How's the girl you met?"

"She's fine, Mother," I said.

Just talking to Mother made me realize I would have to do the right thing. I could live in fear all my life, or I could come forward and do what I had been encouraging Margo to do all along. It gave me a new perspective on her problem, except that I didn't have a murdering mother to worry about.

It was late on Friday night, and Bob Warren was standing guard outside my door. Jim Barnes and Margo and I were watching television when Haymeyer called. "Philip, Hanlon has decided the time has come to fill in Mr. Franklin for his own protection. We've been watching him since you and Margo were threatened, but Hanlon wants him to know what's going on. See how Margo feels about it, and if she gives the green light, we'll talk with him tonight."

Margo was eager for her father to know, and she wanted to see him. "It won't hurt him so much if he knows that Mother didn't really want me killed."

"It's time you were told a few things, too, Margo," Barnes said. "Larry Shipman has gotten next to Salerno since he was extradited to Chicago."

"What did he find out?" Margo asked.

"It took a few days," Barnes said, "but Salerno finally bragged about the fact that he almost killed you. He said that the organization and your mother had been negotiating for a long time on favors the judge could come up with in exchange for the mob's scaring you, and Olga if necessary. He told Shipman your mother had instructed that you be scared but not killed, and that she thought it had been a success."

"She thought?"

"Right. Salerno says he went in there with every intention of killing you."

"What about that women-and-children code?" I asked.

"It exists," Barnes said. "And very few hit men have ever violated it for less than double their normal asking price. Salerno said the organization was going to pay him fifty thousand dollars for this one. He thought it was too good to be true and was a bit careless. He didn't do a final preliminary check on Margo's apartment and found himself facing the dummy."

"Why did he shoot his way out?" I asked. "Wouldn't it have been better for him not to shoot at all?"

"Oh, yeah, and that's the funny part, if any of this can be funny. The same thing happened to Salerno once before. Not a dummy. Just that he smelled a stakeout. There was no target, no dummy, no nothin'. He just dropped his weapon and threw up his hands and all they could get him for was possession of the sawed-off."

"So why did he come out shooting in Atlanta?"

"If he'd known it was a police stakeout, he wouldn't have," Barnes explained. "He thought he'd been set up by the mob."

"Why?"

"He didn't know. There's a lot of jealousy between hit men. Prices and contracts and all that—the news gets around. Every hit man in the East knew Salerno had a big contract and was about to violate the code. When he spotted the dummy and heard the door shut, he figured it was kill-or-be-killed, so he blasted away."

"So they were actually going to go through with killing me."

"Yes, Margo, but your mother doesn't know it. Right now she is pleased with the organization."

"Why did they tell Margo they'd murdered me?" I asked. "And why did Wahl tell me that Salerno never intended to kill Margo and that I wasn't alone in my room?"

"Why not, Philip?" Barnes said. "If those guys ever told the truth, they'd confuse each other. Whatever works, whatever furthers their cause, whatever terrifies you, they'll say it."

"I still take some consolation in the fact that Mother did not intend to have me killed," Margo said.

I pressed my lips tight and shook my head. She noticed.

"I have to agree with Philip," Barnes said. "I suppose it can make you feel better in a way, but remember, she misread them. Why didn't she realize that they might kill you anyway, just to show her who's boss? And now who will they kill to show her their strength? Your father?"

"I want to see him," Margo said.

By midnight Mr. Franklin had been told the entire story and was brought to my room. I was surprised at his height. He was thin, which made him seem even taller and graying. He and Margo held each other tight and long. He was ashen. "You never wanted to believe that Mother was seeing Richard Wanmacher," Margo said.

"I knew all along she was seeing someone, of course, Margo," he said just above a whisper. "I didn't want to admit it to you because I thought you were only guessing. I thought if I denied it all, you might decide you were wrong."

"But I knew, Daddy. I wasn't wrong."

"I know. You were a young woman I treated as a child, and I'm sorry." Mr. Franklin looked helpless, vulnerable. He seemed self-conscious about talking so personally in front of strangers, but he continued.

"You know, Margo, I never dreamed the man was Wanmacher. I detested him, and I thought your mother did too. He was so smug at parties. I made twice as much money as he did, but he treated me the opposite. I couldn't stand that condescending attitude."

"Daddy," Margo said gently, "I've finally gotten over the shock that Mother killed Wanmacher. Do you find it as hard to believe as I did?"

"I don't know," Mr. Franklin said, his shoulders sagging. He still had his coat on. "If he ever treated her the way he treated me, she could have killed him. Richard Wanmacher was one killable person."

"I heard her threaten him, Daddy."

"That's what they tell me. You know, I can just hear him telling her that he couldn't see her anymore. Not that he's sorry, just that she'll get over it eventually. Wouldn't that infuriate you?"

"How do you know what he said?"

"I'm only guessing, honey," he said. "I just know what kind of man Wanmacher was. Arrogant, a smart aleck. Syrupy. I despised him."

"Mr. Franklin," Haymeyer interrupted, "did you ever tell your wife how you felt about Mr. Wanmacher?"

"Dozens of times. I always got the impression she agreed. That's why I never suspected they were seeing each other. I still find it hard to believe. Like I say, I knew there was someone else. There had to be. But not him. He was the cockiest, most arrogant—"

"I think that's what attracted Mother to him," Margo interrupted.

"If it was, she found in him something she never would have found in me."

"What's that?" I asked. Mr. Franklin looked at me. It seemed to bother him that I would ask a question without having been introduced.

He shrugged. "Cockiness," he said. "She always wanted me to act more self-assured, richer than I was. 'Virginia,' I'd say, 'you're always going to be a more impressive woman than I am a man. So you show off and I'll watch.'" He shook his head slowly. "I did always love her, though."

"You still do, don't you, Daddy?"

"No, I don't think I do. I'm not capable of loving a woman who could risk her own daughter's life just to scare her. What if you'd been killed?"

Mr. Franklin broke down and Margo comforted him.

"I'd have never forgiven her," he said.

TEN

The phone rang early the next morning. It was Haymeyer. "We just got a call from Olga Yakovich," he said. "She wants to talk, and Hanlon wants you in on this. I'll be right over to pick you up."

"What we need," Hanlon said back at his office, "is the murder weapon. The proverbial smoking pistol."

"Olga has to have it, doesn't she?" I asked.

"Of course," Hanlon said. "It's her bread and butter."

"Maybe it's what she wants to talk about," I suggested.

"Maybe," Hanlon agreed. "But remember, she can use that gun against us the same way she's using it against Mrs. Franklin."

"How's that?"

"She knows we have nothing solid without it. She can tell us she's got it, but she can demand all kinds of promises from us before she produces it."

"Then you can get her for withholding evidence, right?" I said.

"Very good, Philip," Haymeyer said sarcastically. "Then we've got an old washerwoman for withholding evidence when we want a judge for murder. No, sir, that's not for me. I want that gun with as few promises from us as possible. Once we've got the gun, we've got Franklin."

"I'm not excited about nailing this Yako-what's-her-name on blackmail, Earl," Hanlon said. "I mean, I want her, but I'd make a lot of concessions, even to the point of seeing her stay out of jail, if she'd come up with the gun."

"She might want more than that, Jim," Haymeyer said.

"What more could she want? She's guilty and should get several years!"

"She might want her name left out of the whole thing. Protection for her son. Lots of stuff."

"Boy, I hope not," Hanlon said. "That's all we need."

"Maybe we should go before the grand jury now with what we've got," Earl said. "Let's see if they'll come back with a true bill so we can arrest old lady Franklin."

"Go before the grand jury with what we've got now?" Hanlon echoed. "On what charge?"

"Conspiracy to murder Margo Franklin. Conspiracy to obstruct justice. The murder of Richard Wanmacher."

"Earl, you're dreaming! We have no hard evidence that she conspired to murder Margo. Even Salerno says she thought he intended only to scare Margo. She did conspire to obstruct justice, a serious charge, especially for a judge, though nothing like conspiracy to commit murder. But even the obstruction charge hinges on a mobster's testimony. She could just argue it is an attempt by the mob to get her because she's an honest judge."

"You're right, of course," Haymeyer said, seeming disgusted with himself. "Maybe we should forget the conspiracy charge for now and go after her on the murder."

"All we've got on that one is Margo's word," Hanlon said. "And right now something else is sticking in my craw, Earl. Mr. Franklin seems to have had more of a motive to kill Richard Wanmacher than his wife did. We may need to rethink this whole case."

My mind whirled. Everything had pointed so clearly to Mrs. Franklin, but when I stopped to think about it, how did I really know it wasn't her husband? How could Margo know? Maybe he was in this with Wahl to get revenge on his wife and to eliminate a judge who was troublesome to the mob.

Hanlon was continuing to outline strategy. "The first thing we have to do is talk with Olga," he said. "If she's ready to talk, there's no telling what we may learn."

Hanlon and Haymeyer agreed to let Larry Shipman and

me go along to see Olga. "Yeah, let's really scramble her brain," Hanlon said. "I may regret it, but I'd like to let her see that we mean business and that the best she can do is to tell all, produce the gun, and hope for the best." We stopped by the jail to pick up Shipman and headed for Olga's.

"If you're ready to talk, I'm ready to listen," Hanlon said when she opened the door. "You will either confirm what we already know, or I will begin litigation against you."

"Litigation?" Olga repeated, frowning. Her eyes studied each of us. Larry Shipman could barely keep a straight face. With less a stake in this than any of us, he was simply enjoying the tension, the drama. He seemed to be writing his story in his head.

"I want not to talk to so many," Olga said. "I will talk to you and you." She had pointed to Hanlon and me. "You nice to my Jon," she told me.

Olga took us to one of her bedrooms. "I take money every month," she said when she had shut the door.

"Yes, yes, go on," Hanlon said.

"I take money every month because I have gun used to kill lawyer," said Olga.

Hanlon shot me a now-we're-getting-somewhere look and pressed Olga for more information. "Where is the gun? You'll have to turn it over to us, you know. It's a serious offense to withhold evidence in a murder case."

Olga stared at Hanlon, her jaw set.

"Olga, we can't do anything for you without the gun."

"What I get if I give you the gun?"

"We'll do everything we can for you."

"Want guarantee."

"We've got enough on you now to put you away for years," Hanlon said, his coldness catching me off guard.

"I not say anything more unless I get guarantee. I want no jail, no name in papers, no harm to my son, no nothing."

"You don't think you should have to pay for your crime?

You have withheld evidence in a murder case. You have blackmailed Mr. Franklin. You have virtually stolen the money you've spent on this place and on your son's education."

"Nothing," Olga said, not batting an eye at the mention of Mr. Franklin. "I want guarantee nothing happen to me."

"I can guarantee a lot will happen to you if you don't tell us, Olga. I will charge you with what you have already admitted voluntarily. I have not forced you to say this. You have not been under arrest, but I will put you under arrest if you don't tell us."

"Olga watch TV," she said. "Nothing I say so far can hurt me. Olga have rights."

"You're right," Hanlon said. "You also have my phone number."

Hanlon, Haymeyer, Shipman, and I went back to Hanlon's office. "Where would Olga stash the gun?" I asked.

"Anywhere," Haymeyer said. "If she were smart she'd put it in a safe deposit box."

"If she were really smart," Hanlon said, "she'd have kept it in that apartment all these years, or maybe even in her purse. No one would suspect."

"You know, that gun is not only her meal ticket but her life insurance," Haymeyer said. "The murderer has to want her silenced, but can't do a thing as long as that gun remains hidden."

"If Olga were really stupid—" Shipman began.

"Which she is—" Haymeyer said.

"—if she were really stupid," Shipman continued, "she'd move the gun from wherever she's got it now that the heat is on."

"If she were going to do that, she'd have done it already," Hanlon said.

"Let me finish," Shipman said, sitting on the edge of his chair. "This old broad is shrewd and dumb at the same time.

She'd be better off leaving the gun where no one has seen it all these years, but my guess is that she's moved it."

"To where?"

Shipman waved both arms. "I'm getting to it, just listen. What would be the most desperately stupid thing for her to do right now?"

"I thought *you* were going to tell *us*," Haymeyer said.

"I may have to if you don't guess. On the other hand, if you don't guess, it probably isn't worth speculating about. I know it's a long shot. Just a hunch."

Haymeyer and Hanlon looked at each other. I hadn't said much from the time we'd left Olga's apartment, but something was gnawing at me too. I'd been so quiet that Shipman and Haymeyer and Hanlon could have forgotten I was there. It seemed to startle them when I spoke. "Jon," I said. "Jon might talk her into letting him hold the gun."

"Yes!" Shipman shouted, clapping. "Wouldn't that be the most desperately stupid thing for them to do at this point? Maybe Jon lied to us about her kicking him out!"

Haymeyer and Hanlon were already on their feet, grabbing their coats. I sat with my chin in my palm. "She wouldn't," I said quietly. "Wahl's cohorts would have been watching Olga—she's got to know that."

The three men were on their way out. I followed. "What does Olga know about Wahl or anyone else?" Hanlon asked. "She'd be just dumb enough to do this."

Haymeyer hadn't driven so fast with four people in the car before. Several times we narrowly missed jumping the curb on tight corners as he sped north to the Evanston campus.

"It's just a hunch, a long shot," Shipman kept shouting.

"We have to check it out," Hanlon said. "Philip, you'd better pray that we're onto this before Wahl is."

Haymeyer slid onto the sidewalk in front of the dorm, and we ran up the steps to the third floor. A crowd had already gathered outside Jon Yakovich's room. Students milled about, some turned away holding their mouths. My heart sank.

"Oh, no," Haymeyer said. Hanlon swore. Shipman bullied his way past the crowd.

"Police! Clear the way!" Shipman shouted. "Move out!"

The blood covering the floor was already dry. "It's a Fred Medima hit," Haymeyer told Hanlon as he pushed his way through. "Ear to ear with a straight razor while he slept. The kid had only enough time to arch his back in reflex. It threw him onto the floor where he bled to death in a minute."

I kept pressing forward, though I knew I didn't really want to see. I had known this kid—slim, soft spoken, a slight accent. Loyal to his mother. Defiant when talking about her. Now, in an attempt to give him a good life, she had gotten him murdered.

Jon Yakovich's eyes were open. His teeth were bared. His fingers clutched a sheet and a blanket near his neck, where a gaping wound had let his life's blood gush forth. Only landing on his back had kept him from losing more blood. The heart had long since stopped beating, and blood had coagulated on his neck.

"That's how we know who did it," Haymeyer said, pointing to the straight razor. It had been wiped perfectly clean and had been closed and laid beside the victim's head. Plastic overshoes, which had left perfect impressions in the blood, had also been removed and left behind with a pair of surgical gloves.

"It's the arrogant announcement Medima always makes," Haymeyer said. "It's like Salerno's second shotgun blast."

"How can you stand this?" I asked.

"I can't, Philip," Haymeyer said evenly. "That's why I'm here."

"If the gun was ever here, and we all know it was, it's gone now," Hanlon said.

Olga opened her door carefully. "I hoped it was you," she said, studying our faces. "I think something happen to Jon. What happen to Jon?"

"Why?" Hanlon asked.

"I get call, say no more money come. I can say what I want and it not hurt because I not have gun now."

"What did you do with the gun, Mrs. Yakovich?"

"I give it to Jon," she said. She looked at us, her eyes questioning, pleading. I looked away, and she knew. She cried, "All I wanted was guarantee," she sobbed.

"You've got it," Hanlon said.

"Don't want it now," she said. "Don't want nothin' now."

ELEVEN

The color drained from Margo's face when she heard the news. She sat on the bed in her hotel room and trembled.

"I know it's terrible," Haymeyer said.

Margo shook her head. "That was the name," she said, her throat tight.

"What name?" Haymeyer asked.

"That was the name the man used who was here the other night. The one who told me Philip had been murdered."

"He told you his name?"

Margo nodded, tears welling up. She folded her arms and rocked back and forth.

"What name?" Haymeyer persisted.

"Medima," she said.

Hanlon jumped up and began to pace. "I can't believe they sent Medima for a scare job," he said. "Of all the arrogant—"

"They sent Salerno to Atlanta to scare her," Haymeyer reminded him.

"Salerno meant business. Can you imagine Medima stooping to verbal threats?"

Warren and Barnes shook their heads. "Incredible."

"This Yakovich murder was definitely the work of this Medima?" Mr. Franklin asked.

"Definitely," Haymeyer said. "He's so thorough, so precise, and so consistent, no one could imitate it."

"And he was in my room!" Margo sobbed.

"That's it," I said. "This is too much. How much more can Margo take? Let's confront her mother and get this stopped."

Margo rolled onto her side and hid her face in the blankets. "You may have a point there, Philip," Hanlon said. "Margo, listen." She sat up, staring at him through her matted hair.

"Would your mother be capable of ordering a murder like the one you just heard about?"

"How should I know? She let them scare me. She killed Richard Wanmacher. What wouldn't she do? Who knows?"

"Come on, Margo," I said. "I know it doesn't make much sense right now, but there *is* a difference between killing someone in a fit of passion and ordering the mutilation of an innocent college kid."

"I don't know," Margo said. "I just don't know what to expect from her anymore."

"Well, Jim," Haymeyer said, turning to Hanlon, "where does this leave us? Looks like Judge Franklin has the gun, and we have witnesses to protect."

"Let's move them one more time," Hanlon said slowly, his brow wrinkled. "Get them in a suite, all together, with Barnes and Warren taking turns on watch. Salerno thinks Shipman was just moved to a different building in the House of Corrections, so maybe we'll put him back with Salerno and see what we can get."

At midnight we were moved to a small hotel on the Near North Side. It was a dive compared to where we'd been, but the top floor had a suite with three bedrooms and a reading room and was situated perfectly for protection. After we were settled, Mr. Franklin, Margo, Bob Warren, and I just sat. Barnes posted himself in the hall. No one said much, but we were too tight to sleep. We jumped when the phone rang. It was Haymeyer.

"Hanlon just promised Olga complete exoneration if she'll tell her story to a grand jury. She says it's Judge Franklin who's been paying blackmail. She'll tell the grand jury everything this once and the transcript may be used later, but then she's out of it. She never has to talk again."

"Will it work?" I asked.

"Can't hurt," Haymeyer said. "Hanlon had toyed with the idea of just confronting Judge Franklin, but the decision at this point is to get the charges filed. We're going after her for the murder of Richard Wanmacher and conspiracy to obstruct justice."

The next day, though I was exhausted from lack of sleep, Haymeyer agreed to let me go with him to Virginia Franklin's court. His purpose was simply to rattle her a little if he could.

Margo had described her mother, but I could hardly wait to see her. I imagined her hard, tough, weatherbeaten, sophisticated. I was wrong on almost all counts.

We sat near the back and waited for her entrance. Haymeyer explained the case to me quickly. It was a stock scandal; a broker was charged with fraud.

"All rise!" My heart jumped. We stood and I stared as she walked in. Her robe made her look even tinier than her five feet, two inches. She didn't look nearly Mr. Franklin's age but could have passed for forty. Her black hair was up, expensively done. Her complexion was perfect. She looked soft, loving, motherly. She smiled slightly as she sat down.

I couldn't take my eyes off her. She was a picture of professionalism, class, sophistication. She spoke gently, but steadily. "I believe you were calling a witness when we recessed yesterday, Mr. Trine." I wouldn't have been more surprised if she had shouted obscenities.

Haymeyer said something to me, but I ignored him. I was captivated. Virginia Franklin had to show some evidence of the character Margo had described, but she didn't.

"Want to meet her?" Haymeyer asked.

I answered without looking at him. "Would Hanlon approve?" I asked. "Is she supposed to know I'm in town?"

"Would I suggest it if Hanlon disapproved? I'll tell her you're a friend of mine. She already knows Philip Spence is in town, but she won't know you're Philip Spence."

Judge Franklin was listening carefully to the lawyers and the witnesses, her eyes following the conversation. She took notes occasionally but never looked away from the speakers. She sat with her back perfectly straight.

"Court will break for lunch soon," Haymeyer said. "Let's go back to her chambers and see if we can greet her."

"What will she think about your being here, knowing you're on her case?"

"It will blow her mind, I hope."

We waited near the door to her chambers with the deputy bailiff, a friend of Haymeyer. "She's going to stop this trial this afternoon," the bailiff said. "Told me so herself. She says she's gonna hafta insist that the prosecutor come better prepared to her courtroom."

"She'll just stop the trial?" I asked. "Doesn't she have to wait until the defense moves for a dismissal?"

"You'd think so now, wouldn't ya?" the bailiff said. "But I seen her stop a trial herself more'n once. Did it here not too long ago in the Tony Salerno hearings."

From inside the chambers we heard a door open and close as the judge entered from the courtroom. "Your Honor, Mr. Haymeyer is here to see you, ma'am," the bailiff said, knocking.

"One moment, please," she said, lyrically. In just seconds she opened the door. Her robe had already been put away and she wore a skirt, blouse, and blazer. "It's so good to see you again, Earl," she said, taking Haymeyer's hand and looking him squarely in the eyes. "And who is this young man?" If she'd had an accent I'd have sworn she was a Texas socialite, the perfect hostess. Not a trace of hardness, suspicion, or bitterness. She was one charming and attractive woman.

"This is Bobby Boyd, Virginia," Haymeyer lied. "He's a law student from Ohio State and is visiting to get some exposure to the courtroom."

"How nice," Mrs. Franklin said, taking my hand. She was so soft. She seemed sincerely interested in me.

"It's a wonderful school," she said, catching me off guard. "Is Clarence Hill still there?"

"Clarence Hill?"

"Yes, in the law school. He's been there for years."

"He might be. I'm in pre-law, so I'm really not fully aware of the law school faculty."

"Greet him for me if you should meet him, won't you?"

"Sure will."

"Will you and Bobby have lunch with me, Earl? I'm about to send out for a sandwich, and I'd so like to visit with you."

I could hardly believe she would ask him, but Haymeyer accepted. Our lunches were delivered from within the building.

"I was sorry I had to throw the Salerno case out," Mrs. Franklin said. "I know how hard you worked on it, Earl. And I wanted to see Wahl lose one for Jim's sake."

"Hanlon was hungry for that one, Virginia," Haymeyer said.

"But you know there wasn't enough evidence there," she said. "It irritated me." She looked directly into his eyes and spoke daintily. "I want as much as anyone to have Wahl and his syndicate connections out of Chicago for good. And I'd like to be responsible for their sentencing. But I cannot allow improper charges to violate justice in my court."

I was stunned. This woman was guilty of murder, yet there she sat, acting virtuous and nearly convincing me, though surely not Haymeyer. She insisted she had done the right thing in spite of her "firm belief that Wahl and Salerno and the likes of such men should be imprisoned." She was "forced to rule in their favor when the evidence simply wasn't there."

My mind reeled. This woman was nothing like I expected. Could Margo be wrong? Could she have misjudged her own mother? *Mr.* Franklin seemed a more likely candidate for a murderer than this woman.

"We're all after the same goal, aren't we, Earl?" she asked, begging the only logical answer.

"Yes, we are," Haymeyer said lifelessly. "You never cease to amaze me, Virginia."

She bit into her sandwich and raised her eyebrows as if to say, "Oh? Why?"

"You're always on top of things. Don't you ever get rattled?"

She waited until she had swallowed. "Oh, my, yes," she said, winking at me. "You know very well"—and here she slowed her speech dramatically—"that I get rattled whenever I encounter shoddy investigative work, lazy research, or insufficient evidence. But I must say, Earl, with you that is a rare occurrence." She entwined her fingers on the desk before her and smiled at both of us. I smiled back.

"She's some kinda woman, huh?" Haymeyer said, as we headed for Hanlon's office.

I didn't respond.

"You were charmed, weren't you, kid?"

"Yes, I guess I was."

"You were supposed to be. You know what I was supposed to be?"

"What?"

"Scared."

"Did she scare you?"

"Yup. She made it clear that she will be not be threatened. She will not be rattled. She will not be intimidated. And we are going to have to build a tight case against her or we won't have a chance. She might even have figured you out with that innocent question of hers about the law prof. She was a trial lawyer once, you know, with a reputation of going for the jugular.

"I'll bet if you looked into it you'd find there is not now, nor has there ever been, a law prof named Clarence Hill at Ohio State or anywhere else. The biggest problem is what I've got to tell Hanlon."

"Which is?"

"That she appears ready to stonewall it."

"How can you tell, Earl?"

"It was obvious. She's well rested. Energetic. She doesn't know her daughter was almost killed. She thinks she was just scared and that everything is going according to plan. She's looking forward to this fight. She's challenging me to come up with hard evidence, because otherwise she'll fight till the end and beat it."

"Could she?"

"You'd better believe she could. We'd better be right on the money, no shortcuts, no assumptions. Just hard evidence."

At Hanlon's office Haymeyer relayed the conversation to his boss. "She was in prime form, huh?" Hanlon said. "I don't know if I like that or not."

"I know I don't like it," Haymeyer said. "Why can't it be easy? Wouldn't you think we could shake her up? We've got everything but the gun. We've got Margo, Olga, and even what Salerno's been telling Shipman."

"It's not enough, Earl, and you know it," Hanlon said. "There's not a judge in this town who would convict a peer of murder without a piece of hardware on the evidence table, and from what you say, there's no chance Virginia Franklin is going to give us a break."

"Not even if she were confronted by Margo?" I asked.

Haymeyer and Hanlon looked at each other. "I really don't think so," Hanlon said. Haymeyer nodded. "This woman is like a bullet in a sponge. Soft on the outside and—"

"I can't believe she could sit there knowing that Earl and her daughter were nearly killed in Atlanta and pretend she knew nothing about it," I said. "She didn't even mention it. She had to know that Jon Yakovich has been murdered. She reads the papers, doesn't she?"

Hanlon and Haymeyer nodded. "She knows her stuff," Haymeyer said. "She's not going to give us a thing."

"Not on her own," Hanlon said. "Shipman got a message to me this morning. He says Salerno has been talking with Wahl, and they're about to blow Virginia's case for her."

"How?" Haymeyer asked. "And why didn't you tell me?"

"How could I? You and Philip have been singing her praises so I can't get a word in."

"So what was Wahl supposed to have told Salerno?"

"Shipman says the syndicate is upset with Virginia for call-ing Olga and for having the gall to read them out about the Yakovich murder. Sure enough, they found the gun in Jon's room, but they're holding it, threatening to call in an anony-mous tip and let us find it so we can add it to Olga's testimony and put Virginia away."

"What are they holding out for?"

"She's throwing out a stock fraud case this afternoon for one of their guys."

"We know," Haymeyer said. "She's bragging that one up herself." He mimicked her sweet voice. "Got to have enough evidence, Earl."

"Won't she try to keep Olga from testifying too?" I asked.

"I doubt it," Hanlon said. "But we've got Olga in safekeep-ing anyway. Once she gets her testimony on the record, she can leave town. The irony now is that Virginia Franklin is no longer being milked for three thousand dollars a month by a pathetic old housekeeper. She's being blackmailed for the freedom of syndicate goons. Where will it end?"

"I'm more encouraged than when I came in here," Hay-meyer said.

"Why?" I asked.

Hanlon smiled.

Haymeyer answered. "In a very real sense, my boy, we've got a talented bunch of terrorists on our side. It's Jimmy Hanlon's office and the Chicago organization against her honor, Virginia Franklin."

"I might bet on Mrs. Franklin," I said. "Anyone who can be that low and come off that sweet has got to be somethin' else."

"That she is, Philip," Hanlon said.

Olga's testimony before a secret grand jury that afternoon came tearfully and haltingly. It took more than four hours. "It rang clear as a bell," Hanlon said grimly. "We'll know the ju-ry's decision soon, but there's not a doubt in my mind. We'll get a true bill calling for Virginia Franklin's arrest so we can file charges."

"What then?" I asked.

"Then she finds herself a lawyer and fights our motion for a change of venue."

"Why would you move for a change of venue?"

"We'll maintain that every judge in Chicago will be sympathetic and should disqualify himself. She'll fight it, and we'll be thrilled when she wins. While it's true that most of these judges would protect her, they'll turn on her like scorned lovers if hard evidence comes into the picture. Then we'll be in the driver's seat."

"Won't she figure that out in advance?" I asked.

"Ouch," Hanlon said. "You just heard an ingenious plan from a brilliant U.S. attorney. Give me some credit, kid. This Franklin is shrewd, but she's never tangled with me before." Hanlon thumped his chest with his thumb and grinned. He was only half kidding. He looked forward to the fight as much as Judge Franklin did.

"Will you give the syndicate anything in exchange for helping?" I asked.

"Not a chance," Haymeyer said. "You give breaks to the first timers, like Olga. We'll give the syndicate nothing. Hang it. They'll lead us to Virginia, and she'll lead us to them."

TWELVE

"I have this incredible feeling," Margo told me the next morning. "I've been praying and reading and thinking, and I feel a deep sense of security."

"I wish I did," I said. "I'm finding it easier to pray now that I'm in danger, but as for security—"

"*You're* the veteran Christian," she chided gently. "You should be telling *me* where security comes from. My family's been devastated for years, so it's not like I just lost it. I have new security in God, and in you, I hope."

I cupped her face in my palms. She looked tired. "You're gonna be a good Christian," I said. She smiled.

"I want to grow," she said. "If I didn't have all this on my mind, I think I could really get into it."

"I can't concentrate on anything either. Especially after meeting your mother."

"She's something, huh?"

"She's something."

Barnes had been chatting with Mr. Franklin in the hall so we could be alone for about ten minutes. He knocked and entered. "Haymeyer was just here," he said. "The grand jury is not happy."

"You're kidding."

"No. They don't like the fact that Olga will not testify in an actual trial, and especially that there is no weapon. Haydon was really hassled for coming in with so little. Margo may have to testify."

"So *little?*" Margo said. "Didn't Olga tell them everything?"

"Sure, but why should they believe her? There's no proof the money she's been getting all these years came from your mother. Without the weapon, the grand jury doesn't want to ask for charges to be filed against a judge, especially one of the stature and reputation of Virginia Franklin."

"I can't testify against Mother. I could have when I thought she wanted me killed, but not now," Margo said. "I don't want to. I want to keep out of this. And don't think it's just because she's my mother. I'm scared. For Daddy, for Philip, even for Olga. It seems they'll stop at nothing."

"The grand jury said that without the testimony of Salerno or Wahl or you, Margo, they didn't want to open a can of worms."

"What does Hanlon plan to do?" I asked.

"I think he wants to talk Margo into testifying."

"Is there any way I can avoid it?" Margo asked when Hanlon and Haymeyer arrived late in the afternoon to persuade her to testify.

"There's one possibility," Hanlon said. Haymeyer and Barnes edged closer. Warren was standing guard outside. Mr. Franklin sat on the floor, his back against the side of a bed. "We could tip off Mrs. Franklin. It may backfire, but I think it's a chance we have to take. If she thinks the case is about to become public knowledge, it may force her into some sort of a defense, regardless of her cool facade."

The phone rang. I answered and handed it to Hanlon. "Are you certain?" he said. "Wait until Earl Haymeyer and I can join you. Don't touch anything. No, we have Mr. Franklin right where we want him. He's in our custody on another matter." Hanlon hung up, a grin on his face.

"We've got our break!" he said, clapping. "Barnes, get to Shipman and find out what Salerno is saying. Earl, come with me. That was Ewald from the office. Someone called in an anonymous tip. They say we'll find the Wanmacher murder weapon in George Franklin's car."

Mr. Franklin stood quickly. "What?"

"It means they've played into our hands, if it's true," Haymeyer said. "It sounds as if your wife talked them into using the gun to implicate you so the heat would be off her. They want the attention off her too, because if her reputation suffers, so will all their favors in court."

"But won't the gun implicate me if it's found in my car?"

"We'll worry about that later. Right now we just want to prove that the gun is the one that killed Wanmacher. That'll be the biggest break we've had in this case in years. Then our suspects, instead of being person or persons unknown, will be you and Mrs. Franklin and Olga and Margo, or someone who might have stolen that gun from your home in Winnetka."

"Now *I'm* a suspect?" Margo said.

"Technically," Hanlon said. "Now all we have to do is establish alibis for anyone with a motive."

"First," Haymeyer said, "we have to make sure we've got bona fide evidence."

Hanlon stood and put on his coat. "Right." As he opened the door he casually turned back to Mr. Franklin, now sitting on the bed. "By the way, sir, we need your permission to search your car."

Mr. Franklin waved at him. "Get out of here," he said. "You've got it."

"Can I go?" I said.

"If you hurry, loverboy," Haymeyer said. I winked at an unsmiling Margo. She mouthed a soundless goodbye. I could sense Hanlon and Haymeyer's excitement as we drove to Mr. Franklin's apartment house about ten blocks north.

"I've got to hand it to Wahl," Hanlon said. "Pretty crafty of him to have his boys plant the gun while we've got Mr. Franklin. We gave them the perfect opportunity, and we didn't even plan it."

"Don't say that, Mr. Hanlon," Haymeyer said in his weak British imitation. "I was about to take credit for it."

Ewald and Davis, two young agents from Hanlon's office,

were already in the underground garage at the apartment building. They stood by Mr. Franklin's car. Hanlon tossed a huge key ring to Davis who began trying the various keys. "We're too nervous," Hanlon said.

Haymeyer shot him a double take. "Why?"

"We should have just asked George Franklin for his keys."

"Of course," Haymeyer said, sticking his tongue between his teeth and stifling a laugh. "Here we stand, breaking into the car of a man we have in custody." Ewald and Davis laughed too, but I felt spooked. I shivered and wished we could get on with it. Then the lock popped.

"We'll even let you guys do the looking," Hanlon said, "but when you find the gun just let it lie. I've got a nice Baggie from the crime lab, and I'll sack it myself."

Davis opened the hood and Ewald the trunk while Haymeyer edged toward the front passenger door and peered through the window to the glove compartment. "Come on, Earl," Hanlon said. "Let them find it. Haven't you had enough fun in your career?" Hanlon was enjoying himself. "Save the glove box till last," he said. "That's where it's going to be. Give me a complete search of the car, but save that glove box till last."

The agents removed the spare tire and pulled up the matting in the trunk. Inside the car they looked under the floor carpets and yanked out the backseat bench. Ewald slipped a glove on his right hand and felt under the dashboard. "Nothing," he said to Hanlon. "You want to check the glove compartment yourself?"

Hanlon shook his head, but Haymeyer stepped forward. "I will."

"Now, Earl," Hanlon said. "Let these guys do their jobs. Unlock the glove compartment, boys."

Haymeyer looked embarrassed. Hanlon wanted to see the gun as much as he did, but the United States attorney wanted to savor it. Both stared in when Davis shone his flashlight into the compartment. There was no gun. Hanlon swore. He pushed Haymeyer out of the way and grabbed Davis's flashlight. "Let me in there," he snapped.

He reached into the glove compartment and swept maps, pencils, note pads, a screwdriver, and a change purse out onto the seat with one motion. The compartment was clean. He slammed it shut and lay on his stomach on the front seat, reaching underneath and groping in the darkness. He yanked at the carpeting.

Backing out of the front seat, he hit his head on the roof. He flung the front door shut and climbed in the back, ripping out the bench seat again and looking in vain for the .22. Haymeyer thrust his coat back and jammed his fists on his hips. He walked to the front of the car and slowly raised his right hand and crashed it down on the hood. He swore.

Hanlon was out of the car. "They're loving every minute of this," he said, lips pursed. "They're probably watching. Keep your eyes open."

"And we thought we were so close," Haymeyer said. He turned to Agent Ewald. "Call this number and get permission from George Franklin to search his apartment. We'll wait for you at his door. It's seventeen D."

"Let's not be stupid," Hanlon said, already cool. "This could be a setup. Let's not just barge in."

Haymeyer suggested that Hanlon take the elevator to the seventeenth floor while he and I and Davis took the stairs to guard against any surprise. We stopped to rest at the eighth and fifteenth floors, and when we came down the hall on seventeen, Hanlon was waiting just off the elevator. "Stay here," Haymeyer told me. I was puffing and scared. I backed up against the wall and watched from three doors away.

Hanlon got a nod from Ewald on the permission from Mr. Franklin. Haymeyer stationed the two agents on either side of the elevator. "Better stay away from the door," Haymeyer whispered to Hanlon, who never carried a gun.

Hanlon backed away and Haymeyer drew his revolver. He

stood to the right of the door, reached with his left hand, and knocked loudly three times. He pulled his arm back quickly and we all waited. I heard nothing—not even a breath. Earl waited about thirty seconds and knocked again, his ear near the door, but keeping back far enough to avoid any firing from inside.

Ewald slipped behind Haymeyer and handed him a thin strip of metal. Haymeyer deftly jimmied the lock, turned the knob, and pushed the door open, again stepping back behind the wall. With his pistol out front, he edged into the doorway and flipped on the light. Ewald and Davis followed him and opened the bedroom, bathroom, and closet doors. "It's empty," Haymeyer called out. Hanlon and I joined them.

It took over an hour to go through the pockets of all of Mr. Franklin's clothes. Hanlon was angry. Haymeyer was determined. I moved a pair of old shoes so I could look deeper into the closet and noticed that one shoe felt heavier than the other. I put them next to each other on the bed and called for Earl. Everyone hurried into the room.

"One of those shoes has something in it," I said, backing away as if the shoes were contaminated.

"It's probably a sock," Hanlon said.

Haymeyer picked up one shoe. He hit it on the toe end. Nothing. He tossed it back into the closet. Taking the other shoe carefully in his hands, he sat on the bed. "Uh-huh," he said, looking at Hanlon. "We've got something here."

Something was stuck deep in the toe end of the shoe. Haymeyer tapped it twice but it didn't move. He held the shoe up to the light and peeked in the end. "It feels hard." He shook the shoe and tapped it two more times. When he squeezed the sole from both sides and held the shoe vertically, heel down, the obstruction was freed and slid into view. A *Smith & Wesson .22.*

"Bingo," Hanlon said quietly as Haymeyer looked up and into each face.

The Chicago crime lab called Hanlon four hours after the gun had been delivered. The weapon was clean of fingerprints, had not been fired for years, had one empty shell, and a test bullet had markings that matched the markings on the bullet found in Richard Wanmacher's skull. The gun was registered to George Franklin.

"We've got our murder weapon, but the grand jury won't like where we found it," Hanlon said.

Meanwhile, Larry Shipman had been playing up to Salerno, flattering, idolizing, baiting; Salerno had eaten it up. He was keeping Larry up to date every day. "Salerno says the plant was the old lady's idea," Barnes reported.

"Maybe she's not so smart as we thought," Hanlon said.

"I don't know," Haymeyer countered. "If I were her, I'd want someone other than the organization to have that gun, and I'd want them to find it just where we found it."

"Salerno told Shipman that the old lady insisted on the plant in exchange for future favors," Barnes said. "Whatever that means."

"It could mean a lot of things," Haymeyer said. "Who knows what they've got on the docket? Maybe a raft of syndicate trials are in the works."

"That's not all," Barnes said. "Salerno told Shipman that the bartender at Mr. Franklin's favorite watering hole is going to swear that on the night of the murder he heard Franklin vow to kill Wanmacher."

"Where were you that night?" Haymeyer asked Mr. Franklin.

"When was it again?"

"November eleventh, nineteen seventy."

"I couldn't tell you, but I've been in *The Place* bar almost every evening for the last ten years, so that's a good bet. I know the bartender well, and I can't believe he's going to testify I talked about Wanmacher."

"I wouldn't be too sure," said Barnes. "According to Salerno, the place belongs to the syndicate."

"If he does say that, he's lying. I never bad-mouthed Wanmacher to anyone but Virginia, and even then I had no idea she was seeing him. I might have been capable of killing him, had I known, but I didn't."

"Of course you didn't, Daddy." Margo was crying. "How is this thing going to end?"

No one knew, so we said nothing. Margo's question rang in our ears and haunted us for the next three days. Mr. Franklin listened courteously as Margo told him that God loved him and would carry him through this. "Your mother always said my job was my god, honey," he'd say, at least once a day. "I guess she was right."

"Do the people who work for you know where you are now?" Barnes asked Mr. Franklin one day, just making conversation.

"Only Bernie. He's my right-hand man. He always knows where I am. I'm nothing without Bernie. He won't tell anyone. Watches out for me like a mother hen. Everyone else thinks I'm on vacation."

"Would Bernie know where you were the night Wanmacher was murdered?" Barnes asked, his mind working double-time.

"It wouldn't surprise me. He's got a memory for things like that. I'll bet he'd know where he was when he first heard about it. That's the kind of a guy he is."

Barnes grabbed the phone. "It'd be something if I helped break this case, wouldn't it?" He smiled and looked at each of us. It wasn't just the recognition he wanted. Margo and I had decided that Jim Barnes cared a lot about us. "How do I get ahold of Bernie?"

Mr. Franklin dug out his own business card. "Just ask for him at this number."

"Bernie? This is Jim Barnes, special agent in the office of U.S. Attorney James A. Hanlon. Listen carefully, please. I am with your boss, Mr. Franklin. He tells me you have a sharp memory for detail. Before answering, I want you to listen to my question two ways. Whichever jogs your memory, answer it. This is very important to Mr. Franklin and could help us a great deal.

"I want to know if you have any idea where Mr. Franklin was on the night of November eleven, nineteen seventy. Now, don't answer yet. I know your memory isn't quite that good. Let me ask it this way. Now, think. Are you familiar with the Richard Wanmacher murder? . . . Good. I want to know if you can remember where you were when you first read or heard about it." Barnes kept his ear to the phone for a moment, then wheeled around and frowned at Mr. Franklin. "He wants to talk to you. He remembers, but he doesn't want to tell me."

George Franklin took the phone. "What is it, Bernie? . . . Oh, that's right! You were with me. . . . No, it's all right. Listen, tell Mr. Barnes here. It's OK, Bernie. It's great. Tell him."

Barnes was ecstatic. "You'll swear to this in court if necessary? . . . Super! Now don't tell anyone anything, not about this call, not about anything."

"Well, where were you?" Margo asked when neither Barnes nor her father offered any information. Mr. Franklin cocked his head. Barnes shook his.

"I'm sitting on this one," he said. "I'm gonna hold it as our ace."

"Even from us?" I demanded. "Come on, Jim, this is stupid. You can tell us. Why can't you tell us?" I was livid. So was Margo.

"*You're* going to tell us, aren't you, Daddy?"

"Not unless Jim here gives the OK."

"Come on, Jim," Margo and I said in unison. He just grinned.

It was his, all his, and he wanted to tell Haymeyer and Hanlon. His chance came when they arrived early that evening. He hustled them into the empty room and all we could hear was Hanlon smacking his hands together and Haymeyer asking if he'd checked it out. "No," Barnes said. "I just believed him."

They came back into our room. "It's not a matter of doubting his story, Jim," Haymeyer was saying, irritated. "It's just a matter of being sure. And there's only one way of being sure. Check it out."

Barnes took the phone behind the door and did whatever checking he hadn't done with whatever source he'd been reminded of.

"Why can't we know?" I asked Hanlon.

"The fewer who know, the better," he said.

"Who would I tell?"

"Maybe Mrs. Franklin."

"I'm going to see her again?"

"Tomorrow."

"Why?"

"Because we're going over there to mess her mind a little."

"Haymeyer and I already tried that once, remember? It didn't seem to bother her in the least."

"Well, it'll bother her tomorrow," Hanlon said. "We're going to ask her to appear before a grand jury to tell why her former husband might have had a motive to kill Richard Wanmacher."

"Can't I know before we go what you found out about Mr. Franklin?"

"No."

We visited Mrs. Franklin at her home the next afternoon.

She greeted each with a smile and a nod and a mention of his name. "Earl. *Philip.*" So the masquerade was over and we were into the heavy stuff. She knew me, as she had all along.

Mrs. Franklin asked us to sit down, and pulled her long lounging gown up under her and sat on the couch. She was totally collected.

"I think you know why we're here," Hanlon began.

"You're going to have to tell me," she said, smiling, and I knew she wanted to add, "just like you'll have to work for every other tidbit in this case."

"We're here to ask you to testify for us. I want you to tell the grand jury why your former husband might have had a motive for killing Richard Wanmacher."

Virginia Franklin never flinched. "I had heard, of course, that George was somehow implicated in the murder. How did you come to suspect him?"

"An anonymous tip led us to his place, where the murder weapon was found. Everything matched."

"Well, I'm afraid I won't be of much help to you, Jim," Mrs. Franklin said. "I can think of no reason why George would have wanted to murder Mr. Wanmacher. They were only casual acquaintances, and George never had anything but good things to say about him as I recall."

Hanlon sat dumbfounded, trying desperately to take it all in stride. He had expected Mrs. Franklin to appear shocked that George had been accused, but to admit quickly that she had always wondered.

"He didn't suspect that you were seeing Wanmacher?" Hanlon tried, putting into Judge Franklin's mouth the words he had so badly wanted to hear.

"Seeing Mr. Wanmacher?" Virginia repeated. "Did George say that? I never saw him, as you put it, and if George thought I did, he was wrong. Our marriage had ended long before Mr. Wanmacher was murdered, as I recall. Anyway, Mr. Wanmacher was a married man."

She said it as if she were insulted that Jim Hanlon would dare to accuse her of seeing him. By calling me by name, she had as much as admitted that she knew what was going on, but she was giving Hanlon nothing. Framing Mr. Franklin was her idea, but now she refused to help put him away.

"Well, there's no reason to call you as a witness for the prosecution then, is there?" Hanlon said.

"You could call me, Jim, but I'm afraid I wouldn't help your case."

On the way back, Hanlon was stony. "Why doesn't she jump at the chance to put him away? It would take the heat off her and she'd be home free. Until we spring George's alibi."

"Maybe it looked like a trap to her, Jim," Haymeyer said. "It was coming too easy, right to her doorstep. Sure, it was her idea, but maybe she didn't expect us to run to it so eagerly. She knows we suspect her. She figured we'd only reluctantly switch to suspecting her husband. When it happened so fast, she smelled a rat."

"You're probably right," Hanlon said, banging his open palm on the steering wheel. "Does she think we'll go ahead and prosecute George?"

"I doubt it," Haymeyer said. "We've got enough on him, especially if that bartender is ready to come forward and testify against him. But she knows we know George didn't do it. The only thing we'd gain by trying him would be to taint her reputation. It would have to come out that she was seeing Wanmacher, and that would hurt her."

"She's got us over a barrel," Hanlon said. "The grand jury is going to insist we file against George, and we'll have to pull his alibi out of the hat now."

"That's it!" Haymeyer said. "She knows nothing about the alibi, so she thinks George will be charged. She can protect her reputation while George is being set up by the bartender. She looks lily white, and we've got the murder weapon, found in his apartment. She can even come to his defense somewhat with that no-motive line of hers, knowing full well that we've got enough to nail him."

"There might be a way to get her," Hanlon said. "Let's have Philip tell her about Mr. Franklin's alibi. How would she react to that?"

Haymeyer was puzzled. "I don't get it, Jim."

"We'll have Philip tell her he got permission from us to see her. He can appear to be foolishly telling her our plans, acting as if she should just turn herself in because we've got her figured out."

"So what will come of that?" Haymeyer persisted.

"I can only hope, Earl. What have we got now? It's only a matter of hours before the press and the public start asking for my head or Mr. Franklin's conviction. We've got to try to rattle her."

"You should know by now that she doesn't rattle."

"But something *has* to get to her."

At Hanlon's office I was briefed for two hours and then taken back to the hotel. Margo was eager to hear what had happened, but I was too tired to talk. Haymeyer filled her in, and I went to bed. The next morning I was to call Mrs. Franklin and tell her that I had been given permission to talk with her about the whole matter. My head was crammed with alternate responses to every possible reaction she might have during our conversation.

I didn't sleep well and often caught myself wide-eyed in the darkness, trying to imagine meeting with her alone. More than once I dozed off, dreaming that I had already called her and that I was now in her living room. I had told her that I knew everything and had asked her if she could tell me how much of it was true. In my dream she sat prettily as usual and smiled at me but would not answer. She looked right through me. I wasn't there. She wasn't real. She didn't breathe or move or blink. She just sat, looking, smiling, silent. Then I would open my eyes and stare again into the darkness and try to pray. *Lord, let this end for Margo's sake.*

Once I woke near dawn and realized that it was Sunday. I wondered if Hanlon and Haymeyer would let me take Margo to church. That possibility made me forget about my meeting with Judge Franklin, but only temporarily.

By 7:00 A.M. I was more exhausted than when I had gone to bed. I showered and dressed and knocked on Mr. Franklin's door. He and Margo were already up.

"How is she?" I whispered.

"She didn't sleep well. You don't look so good either."

"I think I'll just sit around for a while," I said. "Tell Margo I'll see her in an hour or so."

I stuck my head out the door of the suite and said good morning to Bob Warren who was sitting guard in the hall. He gave me a thumbs-up sign. "Good luck today, Philip." I nodded and went back in to the couch in the sitting room between the bedrooms. I left the lights off.

With my hands folded in my lap I sat nearly dozing for about twenty minutes. It was a melancholy morning. Very quiet. Margo tiptoed out. I didn't look up. "How are you?" she said.

"Dead."

She sat next to me and took my hand in hers. "I've been reading my Bible," she said.

Still staring at the floor, I smiled. "That's a good Christian. What were you reading?"

"Psalms."

"I need a psalm today. I'm going to see if I can take you to church."

"I'd like that."

Neither of us spoke for several minutes. I felt lifeless. I was so tired, so mentally drained. Yet I was glad I could try to do something for Margo. As tight as I'd been, and as scared and repulsed as I had been by the danger, I had been through nothing compared to her long ordeal.

I laid my head back on the couch and looked at the ceiling. My breathing was even and deep, as if I were asleep. I was sad for Margo. Poor, sweet Margo, whose nine-year nightmare was coming to life. Despite it all, she was somehow able to be sensitive to me.

Emotion welled up inside me. What a beautiful, beautiful person she had become in just the last few weeks. How could she grow with such pressure?

"I love you, Philip," she said quietly, not raising her head.

It was too much. How could she be thinking of me now? Tears poured from my eyes and rolled over my ears to the back of the couch. Her grip on my hand was steady and she did not move.

I sat up and buried my head in my hands, sobbing. She put her arm around my shoulder and her tears fell on me.

"I'm not worthy of your love, Margo," I said.

THIRTEEN

By 9:00 A.M. our suite was crowded. United States Attorney James A. Hanlon brought Earl Haymeyer and Agents Ewald and Davis to join Jim Barnes and Bob Warren. Larry Shipman had been "released" from jail and came to report on the latest from Salerno, which wasn't much.

Salerno had been strangely quiet for the last two days, except for grumbling that his lawyer, Frederick Wahl, was trying to get him sent back to Atlanta to answer the attempted murder-charges. "It's as if he wants me sent up," Salerno had groused to Shipman. "I'm guilty down there."

"Are you guilty up here?" Shipman had asked him.

"Sure. But with old lady Franklin stonewalling it, they've got nothing on me. If they get me up here, I'm taking Wahl with me. He was there when I got the assignment from Judge Franklin to scare her daughter. And he was the one who put the fifty-G price tag on Margo's head."

Margo winced.

"You sure you want to hear this?" Hanlon asked.

She nodded.

"Maybe we should admit that we're not going to file charges against Salerno right away," Haymeyer said. "To keep from getting shipped back to Atlanta, he might rat on the judge and on Wahl."

"It's a thought," Hanlon said. "Let's see how hard Wahl pushes for his release. I'm sure the whole organization is nervous about having a restless big-mouth behind bars, especially one who sees little hope.

"Anyway, people," Hanlon continued, addressing the group and reminding me of a grade school teacher I'd had in Dayton, "today is a big day. If we can't get Mrs. Franklin to tip her hand, we're going to tip it for her. Earl is heading the strategic end of things, as usual, and he has instructions for everyone."

Hanlon stepped over Mr. Franklin and sat on the couch. Haymeyer began: "Philip will call Mrs. Franklin in about ten minutes and ask to see her at one o'clock at her home. He has already been briefed on how the conversation should go. Right now it all hinges on Mrs. Franklin's availability.

"Agents Ewald and Davis will stay with Mr. Franklin and Margo here. Mr. Hanlon and I will follow Philip in one car as far as the northern limits of Chicago and then we'll circle back. Jim Barnes will pick up the tail there and will follow Philip to Winnetka. Then he'll circle back.

"Bob Warren will be under a blanket in the back of Philip's car and will remain there all the time Philip is with Mrs. Franklin. By following Philip in two separate cars and having Bob in his car, we'll be able to protect Philip from any interference, although we don't expect any.

"Bob will have a radio, so we can contact Philip if we think he's being followed."

I raised my hand. "Any chance I could take Margo to church this morning?"

Haymeyer looked at Hanlon who gave him an it's-your-case shrug. "Let me think about that," Haymeyer said. "If you choose a church in the suburbs it might be a good way for us to test our surveillance plan. I'll let you know.

"Anyway, Philip, when you're through talking with Mrs. Franklin, just head right for Mr. Hanlon's office. We are fairly certain you will be followed from Winnetka, even if you aren't followed on your way there. If these guys don't know where this hotel is by now, there's no sense leading them straight to it."

"They have to know where it is by now, don't they Earl?" Davis asked.

"We've always taken different cars and different routes," Haymeyer said. "But I wouldn't be surprised if they're watching. That's why you and Ewald will stay here. I don't care if they know where we are, as long as they know they can't get to our people.

"It's time for Philip to call Mrs. Franklin. Let's have silence while he's on the phone."

My hand shook as I dialed. As Mrs. Franklin's phone rang for the fourth time I looked up at Haymeyer. "She's got to be there," he said. "Where would she go this early on a Sunday?"

"Certainly not to church," Margo said.

"Franklin residence."

I was surprised it wasn't Mrs. Franklin. "Uh, yes, uh, Mrs. Virginia Franklin, please."

"I'm afraid she's sleeping right now, sir. May I take your name and number?"

"Just a minute," I said, covering the mouthpiece. "It's some woman, the cleaning lady, I suppose. Mrs. Franklin's asleep. Should I leave this number?"

Hanlon shook his head vigorously and barked rapid-fire instructions: "Tell her it's very important to wake Mrs. Franklin. She'll talk to you."

"It's very important that I talk to her," I said. "Could you wake her and tell her it's Philip Spence?"

"I hate to, sir. I have strict orders."

"Tell her that I insisted. I'll take the blame."

"One moment, sir."

My heart pounded. "Be cool," Haymeyer whispered.

"Easier said than—hello? Mrs. Franklin? I'm sorry to bother you so early."

"That's all right, Philip," she said huskily. "I'm embarrassed to be sleeping so late. What can I do for you?"

"I'd like to see you today, if I could."

She hesitated. "Alone? I mean, I'm not sure I understand."

"I have gotten permission to come and talk with you." She didn't respond, and I didn't know what else to say. I glanced at Haymeyer. He clenched a fist to encourage me. "Your daugh-

ter is of mutual interest to us," I said finally. Haymeyer nodded.

"That is true, Philip," she said, immediately cool again. "I
don't know what you want to talk about, but I could see you
sometime perhaps this evening."

"No, I mean like around one o'clock," I said, wincing.

"Oh, you have a schedule?"

"No, I'm sorry. I guess any time you're free would be OK."

"No problem, Philip. I can see you at one. Where shall we
meet?"

"At your house," I said.

"My goodness, you do have it all planned, don't you?"

"I'm sorry," I said. "I—"

"No, no, that's fine, Philip. I'll look forward to seeing you
then."

"I almost blew it, huh?" I said after hanging up the phone.

"No," Haymeyer said. "She knows what's happening. The
fact is that she's not afraid of you. She'll see you any time
anywhere. I don't think she believes this was your idea, which
it wasn't. But I'll bet she'll give you an earful today. With no
one else listening, she might even talk freely about what's
been going on."

"You really think so?"

"Why not? She'll be coy with me or with Hanlon, but she'll
probably tell you anything just to scare you or amuse herself.
Who's going to believe you? She'll just deny it later, if necessary."

"Then what's the point?"

"The point is that if you can get her to admit she's behind
this whole mess, maybe you can start talking about things
that will get to her."

"Like what? I haven't seen anyone ruffle her yet."

"Like me," Margo said.

"Right," Haymeyer said, "Like Margo. We can't be sure.
Maybe this woman is so cold and calculating that she can't be

shaken. And maybe even her own daughter means nothing to her anymore—I'm sorry, Margo, it may be true—but at least it's a chance."

"How about church?" I asked.

"Where?" Haymeyer asked.

We checked the phone book and found a Bible church in Evanston. "How's that?" I asked Haymeyer.

"OK with me. Maybe even perfect. What time would you get out of there?"

"Around twelve-thirty or so, I guess."

"Great. Even if she has tipped off anyone that you're coming, they'll never expect you to leave this early. We'll follow you there, and Barnes can follow you from the church to her house."

"What about me?" Barnes asked.

"Good question, Jim," Earl said. "Can you stay in the car all that time?"

"During church? How long is it?"

"Over an hour," I said.

"What if you and Hanlon dropped me off somewhere en route to the Franklin house and Philip could pick me up on his way from the church?"

"OK," Haymeyer said. "Sounds like we're all set."

Margo stepped close to Earl. "No, we're not all set," she whispered. "I want to go with Philip."

"You are going with him. Then, we'll pick you up in the church parking lot when he heads for your mother's house."

"That's what I mean," she said. "I want to go with him to see Mother."

Haymeyer stared at her. "Margo, please let me handle the strategy, will you?"

"I really want to go, Earl. Why can't I?"

Hanlon caught Haymeyer's eyes from over Margo's shoulder. He spread his palms as if to ask, "Why not?" Haymeyer glared at his boss. "It's your operation, Earl," Hanlon insisted.

"OK, Margo, listen. We have to talk this over, the boys and I. I'm going to come to a decision while you're in church. If I'm in the parking lot, you come with me, understand?" Margo didn't respond. "If I'm not there, you go with Philip."

Margo's look told Haymeyer she was determined to go with me. "Margo," he said, "I don't want trouble from you. You weren't in on the briefings, you don't know what is supposed to be said or not said. You might just blow the whole thing."

"If my name is supposed to rattle Mother, won't my presence rattle her even more?"

"Is that why you want to go?"

Margo sat down wearily. It was hard for her to talk, and the other agents looked away. "I want to go because I miss my mother. All right?" she said. "Is that a good enough reason? I want to see her again."

"I can sympathize with that," Haymeyer said. "But that feeling is going to make you take her side. You're not going to want to see her break down and admit her part in this, are you?"

"Is that what you think she'll do? You've got her underestimated."

Haymeyer was confused. "Are you proud of your mother's deceit?"

"Do you really think Mother will crack?"

"She just might," he said. "I think Philip is ready for her, and I think if anyone can get to her soft spot, he can."

"Why?"

"Because he loves you."

"How do you know?"

"He told us."

Margo looked quickly at me. She couldn't respond. The news had come to her in the form of a begrudging argument.

Haymeyer continued. "If your mother loves you, she'll feel something toward Philip. She'll understand him a little. She'll sense what he feels for you."

"And if she doesn't still love me?"

"Then maybe he can at least make her feel remorse over what she almost did to you."

"I still want to go."

"Why!? Don't you understand?"

"I understand perfectly. You're the one who doesn't understand, Earl. I want to see my mother one more time before I know for sure that she's the person I've hated all these years. When she admits it, when it's all out in the open, I'm not going to know her. She'll spend the first few minutes with Philip just feeling out where he is. She'll be her old charming self. I want to see her at her best one last time. She so seldom cracks. When she does she's going to be devastated, never to charm anyone again, not even in deceit."

"And what about when Philip nails her to the wall? What about when your presence, and his love for you, and his knowledge of the facts, and the news that she almost got you killed, hits her with full force? Are you going to want to be there then?"

"Yes."

"I can't believe it," Haymeyer said, wheeling around. "How can you say that?"

"Because I don't hate her anymore. You can't understand it, but God has forgiven me for hating her. He's helped me understand her a little. I'm still hurt and bitter about a lot of things, but Mother suffered too. Her life wasn't what she thought it would be. She tried to take things into her own hands and she hurt herself, she hurt me, she hurt Daddy, she killed Richard, and ruined his wife.

"She's been suffering all along, but she hasn't been able to tell anyone, like I have, and she'll suffer more. I think most of my suffering is past. When Mother's defenses crumble, what will she have? A virtual stranger in her house, zeroing in on her weak spots, haunting her with what she's done to me."

"So what are you going to do, Margo?"

"I'm going to forgive her." The agents traded glances. They

thought Margo had flipped, and they appeared eager to get to Haymeyer so they could advise that she be tranquilized, or at least kept away from Winnetka. "She'll have to answer for everything she's done. I can't and won't try to stand in the way of that, and I'm not saying any of what she's done was justified. But I have no right to avenge what she's done to me. I want her to know that someone still cares about her."

Haymeyer was speechless. When he finally said something, it was to change the subject. "Just in case I decide you can go, Margo, you'll have to be briefed."

While he filled her in, I tried to talk with Mr. Franklin. He looked sick, sitting on the floor with his chin tucked to his chest.

"Philip, how can she love like that? I never loved anyone that much, certainly not Virginia. I hate her. I hated her when she just bugged me to be more image conscious. I hated her more when we got divorced. But when I learned she'd been seeing Wanmacher, and might have killed him, and then scared Margo and almost got her killed too—"

I put my hand on his shoulder. His words came slowly. "I'll never forgive her for what she's done, and I don't understand how Margo can."

"She can't," I said, "any more than you can or I can. By ourselves, we aren't capable of that kind of love and forgiveness."

"I know I'm not," he said.

"Only God can love like that," I said. He looked away and nodded, signaling the end of our conversation.

At 10:30 Haymeyer finished with Margo and she went to change clothes. "That's some woman you've got there, Philip. I don't like this, but I'm willing to go along with it. If Mrs. Franklin doesn't come around, don't belabor it. I don't think you should be there for more than an hour."

Haymeyer and Hanlon took Bob Warren in their car and gave me the keys to another. Mr. Franklin stayed with Shipman and Ewald and Davis. Barnes was already on his way to the church where he would wait to follow us to Winnetka.

Margo sat close to me in the car on the way to Evanston. "So you love me, huh?" she said.

"Not really, but it sounded like the right thing to say at the time."

She smiled. "This still hurts," she said, suddenly serious.

"I believe that," I said.

While we waited for the service to begin, Margo said it had been a long time since we'd been to church together.

"It just seems like a long time. Do you remember what the sermon was about?"

"Hardly. That was the night I was almost killed. All I remember is praying through the whole evening. I'll be praying all morning this time."

"Me too," I said.

"About what?"

"About confronting your mother, of course."

"Not me. I've already got that one settled."

"Then what'll you be praying for?"

"That Haymeyer will see the wisdom of letting me go with you."

"Why don't you channel your energy into praying for me, then? Haymeyer already told me you could go."

Margo stiffened as we left the church. Haymeyer was in the parking lot. She looked at him defiantly. "I'm going, aren't I?"

"No, Margo, and don't you dare make a scene." He was so forceful that Margo backed down. Haymeyer pulled me away. "We've spotted a tail," he said. "I can't risk Margo's going along. You don't have to go either, you know."

"I'll go."

"Good, but be careful. Don't do anything foolish. Talk straight with Mrs. Franklin; don't take any garbage. You each know exactly what the other is up to, so make sure she understands that. We've already got Warren in your car, so just head up there."

I caught Margo's eye as she walked with Hanlon toward Haymeyer's car. There was no time to say anything. It didn't seem right to leave her that way. I felt incomplete as I pulled out of the lot.

"How you feeling, kid?" I jumped. It was Warren.

"I almost forgot you were back there," I said.

"You better know I'm back here, partner. From what they tell me, you may need me this afternoon."

"Thanks a lot."

"You're just getting straight stuff, Philip. You'll always get straight stuff from me."

"So what's happening, Bob?"

"Well, you were followed to the church. When the car went around the block to find a spot to wait for you to come out, I jumped in here."

Static came from Warren's radio. "Ten-four," he said. "That was Barnes, Philip. We've got ourselves a tail again. Can you see anyone?"

I checked the rearview mirror, as I had all along. "No. Is Barnes sure?"

"Of course, he's sure. And you may never see your tail. That's how good they are. Anyway, they know where you're going. They just want to be sure you're alone."

"Would they have spotted Barnes?"

"It's possible, but remember, he's pulling out of the picture as soon as you're in the driveway. They'll quit worrying about him. I'm their problem, and they don't know about me, I hope."

I was sure I'd be blown away when I left the car to go to the house, and told Warren so. He tried to put me at ease. "They don't want you, kid. Anyway, if they *were* going to hit you, they'd do it inside the house."

"*That* helped," I said.

In spite of his reassurances, I never felt so vulnerable as when I was walking toward the front door. I hardly breathed, my heart pounded, my legs wobbled. I rang the bell. The housekeeper, in her coat, opened the door and greeted me. Then she left.

The overdone hospitality of Virginia Franklin was gone. "Hello, Philip," she said formally as we sat in the living room. "I find it interesting that they sent you in to do battle with me."

"Maybe it's because I love your daughter. Do you?"

"It's irrelevant. What is relevant is how you're going to try to break me. How are you?"

"I just tried. I guess I'm through. If your daughter means nothing to you, what can I say?"

"Not much. But as long as you're here, why don't you tell me how Hanlon's case against me is going?"

"Oh, I imagine you know."

"Yes, I suppose I do. Any new developments?"

"What do you know already, Mrs. Franklin?"

"Well, I know Hanlon's aware of my dealings with Wahl and Salerno. That was rather transparent, but hard to prove." Her eyes danced. "How're they going to prove that one, Philip?" I shrugged. She settled back comfortably on her couch.

"They've got Olga's word on the blackmail money. Again, hard to prove, right?"

I shrugged again. I was appalled. What a contrast she was to the charming woman I had met earlier.

"They've got Margo's word on my affair with Richard. Impossible to prove, in spite of Olga's corroboration. You see, my husband was always ignorant of that relationship. He hasn't got the guts to lie, so he could never testify against me. Who would believe him anyway? If he said it, he would seal his own doom. You know what they've got on him already."

I nodded.

"Well, Philip. Where am I weak? I've got a former husband who still finds it hard to believe that I killed a man. As much as he can't stand me, he's going to pay for my crime. Isn't that nice of him? And I've got a tacky, so-called daughter who thinks her testimony about my midnight ride is going to put me in my place. What do they have on me, Philip? What's going to do me in?"

"Three things," I said, surprising myself with my calm.

"I can't wait to hear them," she said, edging forward. She was loving it.

"First will be the syndicate."

"Oh, come now. Who's going to believe I would deal with such low-down characters?" She was smiling.

"Let me finish." She nodded. "It's not someone finding out about your dealing with them. It's them. They don't like to owe favors."

"They can't help it. They need me."

"You're not letting me finish. I've got three points, and I'm not through with the first one yet."

"Oh, that's naughty of me, isn't it, and me a judge at that. I'm so sorry, Mr. Spence. Please continue."

"The syndicate doesn't need anyone it can't scare. What would you say if I told you that what happened in Atlanta was a mistake?"

"I'd say you were wrong. It worked perfectly according to plan, except that Earl Haymeyer sniffed it out. No harm done. It was a scare job, anyway. Salerno might do some time, but my mission was accomplished."

"Yours was, but Wahl's wasn't."

"Is this point number two?"

"No, we're still on number one. Wahl promised Salerno fifty thousand dollars if he killed Margo."

"Nonsense. Salerno never got fifty for a job in his life. Anyway, he'd never hit a woman. And why would Wahl want Margo hit?"

"To show you where you stood. Wahl had you misjudged almost as drastically as you had him misjudged. He thought your daughter was dear to you and that was the only reason you wanted her scared instead of murdered."

Mrs. Franklin threw her head back and looked at the ceiling. The position of her neck made her sound laryngitic. "You don't know what you're talking about," she said.

"Don't I? Let me ask you something. If your daughter means nothing to you, why didn't you just have her killed? It would have looked like revenge from the mob for past sentences you've handed down. Margo would have been silenced for good. You wouldn't have cared, would you? She's a tacky, so-called daughter, right?"

"Philip, how do you know they were going to cross me and kill Margo?"

"Let's get to point number two, shall we?" I said. She was so seldom frustrated that I wanted to milk it, but she wouldn't let go.

"Tell me how you know this."

She had put me in the driver's seat. "All right," I said. "Through Salerno. He's a big-mouth. One of Hanlon's men got next to him in jail, and Salerno's been singing ever since. He doesn't much like the idea of going back to Atlanta to face attempted murder charges either. He's going to tell about conspiring with you to scare Margo, and he'll implicate Wahl in the process."

"Nonsense. Wahl will call him a liar and so will I. Who would ever believe I conspired with a mobster to scare my own daughter?"

"Maybe you're right," I said. "Margo finds it hard to believe."

"En garde, eh?"

"You're more naive than I thought, Mrs. Franklin. If you think Wahl is with you, why did he promise Salerno a bundle to kill Margo?"

"I still don't believe that one."

"You could take my word for it. But then, what do I know? I'm the one who thought you still had a shred of love left for Margo. Don't you even care to know how she is?"

"Sure. As long as you're here, how is Margo?"

"You're trying too hard, Mrs. Franklin. You're dying for some word from Margo."

She stood. "I'm not! She abandoned me when I needed her. I tried to get close to her, but she kept taunting and accusing."

Something had broken loose in Judge Franklin. She was defending her feelings toward Margo.

"Why do you hate her?" I asked.

"Because she wouldn't respond. I had no one. I tried to make up to her. I bought her things, I paid her way to Atlanta, I started a savings account for her. She left me alone."

"She's sorry," I said. "That's point number two."

"Don't give me that," Mrs. Franklin spit out, turning quickly and facing me. "She can't throw an apology in my face. Who does she think she is?"

"Didn't you just say she abandoned you? She wants your forgiveness."

Mrs. Franklin snorted and threw her head back. She began to speak but just let out a loud sigh. She set her jaw and returned to the couch. As she sat down she hid her face and fought tears. "If I forgive her, she'll have to forgive me." She paused. "And how could she?"

Mrs. Franklin thrust her hands beneath her and sat staring at the floor. I began to tell her of the Margo she never knew. "I met her in the Atlanta Tower," I said. The judge nodded in recognition. "Not in the second-floor restaurant," I said. "On the thirtieth floor. She was about to jump out the window." Mrs. Franklin's shoulders tightened, but still she wouldn't look at me. "I talked her out of it by telling her that Someone loved her, that Someone cared. It was hard for her to believe, but it worked because she wanted so desperately for it to be true.

"I told her that God loved her. Do you want to know what she told me?"

Mrs. Franklin made no response.

"She told me that she started gaining weight when she lost her security at home. She dreamed of the good old days. She'd see you and Mr. Franklin sleeping in separate rooms, treating each other like neighbors, and she'd cry herself to sleep. All she could think of was her childhood. Trips to the zoo with Mommy and Daddy."

"Don't," Mrs. Franklin whispered, but I continued.

"Being carried when she was too tired to walk. Seeing you and your husband look into each other's eyes."

Mrs. Franklin hid her eyes with one hand and waved at me with the other. She'd had enough. I leaned forward. We were sitting directly across from each other, almost knee to knee.

"Well," she said finally, "it was a gallant effort, and I commend you. But I have come too far. I'll not be giving it up this easily." She forced a smile.

"What do I tell Margo? That you refused to forgive her?"

"Just tell her she's not going to con me into asking her forgiveness by pretending that she wants mine."

"You don't have to ask for her forgiveness, Mrs. Franklin. She asked me to tell you that it's yours already, no strings attached. Whether you ask for it or not."

Her lips trembled and she turned her head away. Then her mouth curled into a smirk. "That's just too touching," she said, dripping sarcasm. "I've come this far—I'll keep going."

I stood and began moving toward the door. Mrs. Franklin didn't move. "Don't think you've got me on the ropes, Philip. I'm fully aware that you haven't gotten around to point number three. The first two didn't do me in, as you promised. I want to hear number three."

"I'm embarrassed," I said. "Frankly, I never thought we'd get to three."

"Had me underestimated, did you?"

"For sure," I said. "Anyway, Mr. Hanlon told me that he would have to deliver point number three personally. And he also advises that you have a lawyer present."

"It must be a winner," she said, never missing a beat, though her face still betrayed her cocky tone. "His place or mine?"

FOURTEEN

Amos Chakaris, a former Illinois secretary of state and semiretired lawyer, arrived at Hanlon's office with Mrs. Franklin early in the evening. He was a tall, fat, white-haired man, obviously an old friend of both Mrs. Franklin and James Hanlon. The United States attorney seemed surprised and genuinely pleased to see Chakaris.

Mrs. Franklin showed little surprise at seeing Margo, except to comment on her weight loss. Margo looked as if she wanted to run to her mother and began to cry softly when the judge treated her as if she were a casual acquaintance.

"Now what's this all about?" Mrs. Franklin asked sweetly, as soon as we had all been seated. "And where's everyone else?"

"You know where they are, Virginia," Hanlon said. "And you also know what this is all about."

"You'd better let me speak for you, Virginia," Chakaris said. "Jim, is my client about to be arrested and charged?"

"Yes, unless she chooses to cooperate."

Chakaris appeared slightly amused. He seemed genuinely convinced that Virginia Franklin could not be guilty of anything serious enough to involve the United States attorney. "Virginia has told me nothing, Jim," he said. "What is this, some sort of conflict of interest or complicity?"

Mrs. Franklin smirked at Hanlon behind her lawyer's back. "So you're even going to make it hard on Amos, huh, judge?" Hanlon said.

"Why am I here?" she said, brows raised.

Chakaris leaned close to whisper to Hanlon. "Jimmy, we've known each other a long time. Can't we clear this up without these kids here?"

"They aren't kids. This is the judge's daughter and her boyfriend. They're as involved as anyone. Amos, we're filing charges against Mrs. Franklin for the murder of Richard Wanmacher and conspiracy to—"

Chakaris leaped from his chair and stomped back and forth, rubbing his hand over his mouth. "Why didn't you tell me, Ginny?" he complained. "I can't come in here prepared to represent you unless I hear your side."

"My side of what?" she asked. "What's it all about, Amos?"

Chakaris pulled Hanlon off to the side and demanded to know why Mrs. Franklin hadn't been informed. "She knows," Hanlon insisted. "Can't you see this is a game? We've got her dead to rights. I've got a secret grand jury testimony, a deposition from Margo, and evidence of syndicate involvement."

Chakaris looked at Margo and me over his shoulder and pulled Hanlon into the hall. Mrs. Franklin edged forward and patted Margo on the knee. "So how've you been?" she said. Margo pulled away.

"I don't know you," she said.

"You never have," Virginia said. Margo hung her head.

"You are too much," Haymeyer said.

"Hello, Earl," Mrs. Franklin replied kindly.

I couldn't believe it. She casually lit a cigarette, crossed her legs, and let her shoe dangle from her toe.

Chakaris and Hanlon returned after several minutes. "I want to talk to my client," the old lawyer said.

"I have nothing to tell you," Mrs. Franklin told him. "I'm totally in the dark on this, and I simply want to go home as soon as you clear it up."

"Then maybe I should tell *you* what it's all about," Chakaris said.

"I'd rather hear it from Mr. Hanlon," she said, smiling.

Chakaris spread his hands, palms up, and shrugged. "Do your thing, Jim."

Hanlon turned to Haymeyer. Earl stood and faced Mrs. Franklin who remained seated.

"Mrs. Virginia Franklin?" Earl began. She cocked her head

in affirmation. "You are under arrest for the murder of Richard Wanmacher and for conspiring to obstruct justice by contracting with Frederick Wahl and Antonio Salerno to keep Margo Franklin from coming forward with evidence in a murder case. You have the right to remain silent."

"I am quite aware of my rights, Earl, thank you very much. My legal counsel is here, and I waive the right to silence."

"Not so fast, Virginia," Chakaris said.

Mrs. Franklin turned icy. "I'm not guilty, Amos, and I will not go to trial. I want countercharges filed. I am being charged without evidence, and I want to see Mr. Hanlon suffer for this. I happen to know that my former husband murdered Richard, and that Jim here has the evidence to prove it."

"Yes, Mrs. Franklin, I do have some evidence here against your former husband," Hanlon said. "Would you care to see it?"

The judge eyed him warily, then shifted her eyes to Chakaris who sat down and turned away from her.

"What is it?" she asked.

"Do you know Bernie?" Hanlon said, toying with her.

"Bernie who? You mean George's Bernie? Of course. He'll do anything for George. Run for his paper, run for his slippers, just like a puppy."

"Well, Bernie remembers where he heard about the Wanmacher murder."

"Good for Bernie," Mrs. Franklin said, attempting to regain her composure. "All George ever talked about was Bernie's memory." She dragged on her cigarette, but kept her squinting eyes on him.

"He got the word about the murder before the newspapers did, Virginia," Hanlon said gently. "He got the word from a desk sergeant at the sixteenth precinct station. Know why he was there?"

Mrs. Franklin waved him on.

"He was bailing George out of the drunk tank. George had

been there from two hours before the murder until nearly dawn. I have here a copy of the log sheet, verifying that he was behind bars while Richard Wanmacher was being murdered."

Hanlon held the log sheet before Mrs. Franklin's eyes. She looked past it to his face, her lips tight. She whirled to face Margo. "All right!" she said. "I can't protect you any longer!" Margo's mouth dropped open. "She did it," Mrs. Franklin said. "She thought Richard had broken up our family and—"

"It won't wash, Virginia," Haymeyer broke in. "We have Olga's testimony that Margo never left the house that night. And we have both Olga's and Margo's word that you left in plenty of time and were gone long enough to have shot Wanmacher."

Chakaris stood and thrust his mammoth hands into his pockets. He sat again when Margo stood and faced Mrs. Franklin.

"Mother, you are killing me," Margo said, on the verge of tears. "You wanted me scared into silence and almost got me killed, and now I wish you had. I thought the last nine years were a nightmare, but this is unbelievable. What will you come up with next?

"Doesn't it matter to you that you're pulling this on your own daughter? I knew you when you were warm and good. What are you now? When I realized what you had done and how far you had gone to cover up, I remembered the good times and took some solace in them. Now what am I to do? You're erasing my good memories. All I see is this woman I don't know. Do you know my mother?"

Mrs. Franklin looked at her quizzically.

"I used to call her Mommy," Margo continued. "She loved me and she loved my daddy and she was warm and kind and good. I haven't seen her for years. Do you know her?"

Mrs. Franklin bit her lip. She trembled.

"Mother, no one believes you. What you need is support and forgiveness. And you have it."

"I do? From where?' Mrs. Franklin's eyes were ablaze.

"From me."

"Have I *hurt* you?"

"What do *you* think?"

Mrs. Franklin put out the cigarette she'd been ignoring. She spoke slowly, "I don't think, Margo. I haven't thought for years. When I think, I hurt. When I think of what your life must be like, I hurt."

"Well, I've hurt too, Mother. And I'm hurting now. I thought I was hurting before, but I didn't know the meaning of the word. Seeing you like this hurts me more than anything."

"Stop! Why are you doing this to me, Margo? Don't you think I know what I've been doing? How much do you think I can take? Sure you've been hurt, but look what I've been through. What do I have left? I know I'm grabbing at thin air, but air is all I've got. Now you stand here and tell me I'm not what I used to be. That I'm killing you by being this way. Well, I ask you, what am I supposed to be like? What is the dignified thing to do now?"

Margo stared at her mother. "I want you to accept my forgiveness."

Virginia's face was contorted. She shook her head. "You can't forgive me," she said. "You simply cannot. I won't let you. It's impossible."

"You don't want my forgiveness?"

"What will it do for me? Your forgiveness would belittle me—crush me. I would be humiliated even more, if that's possible."

"But I offer love."

"Margo, you're loving my memory. You can't love me now."

"I can and I do."

"You can't love me!"

"God is loving you through me." Margo's tears were flowing freely now. "I hate the things you do and I pity you. But God lets me love you in spite of myself."

Mrs. Franklin broke down. I thought I'd never see her cry. "Margo, Margo," she said. "What should I do?"

Margo embraced her. "Give it up, Mother. Just give it up."

"I'll suffer. I'll pay. You know I'll be sentenced. And I'll be alone."

Margo held her closer.

"You'll never be alone. God loves you, Mother. I love you. You'll always have me."

And Margo would always have me.

ABOUT THE AUTHOR

Jerry Jenkins is a widely published author of biographies and fiction. He has written the biographies of Orel Hershiser (on the *New York Times* Bestseller list for nine weeks), Meadowlark Lemon, Hank Aaron, Walter Payton, B. J. Thomas, Dick Motta, Luis Palau, and Deanna McClary.

Many of Jenkins' ninety books have topped the religious best-seller lists.

His writing has been published in *Reader's Digest, The Saturday Evening Post,* and virtually every major Christian magazine.

Jenkins is writer-in-residence at Moody Bible Institute. Born in Kalamazoo, Michigan, Jenkins lives in the country near Zion, Illinois, with his wife, Dianna, and their three sons, Dallas, Chad, and Michael.